THE PREORDAINED

By the same author:

The Heritage, Trafford Publishing
A Price for Rainbow, NNI Publishers (Nigeria)

THE PREORDAINED

Abdulaziz Anako Fache

Book Guild Publishing
Sussex, England

First published in Great Britain in 2008 by
The Book Guild Ltd
Pavilion View
19 New Road
Brighton, BN1 1UF

Typesetting in Baskerville by
Ellipsis Books Ltd, Glasgow

Printed in Great Britain by
CPI Antony Rowe

A catalogue record for this book is available from
The British Library.

ISBN 978 1 84624 232 8

For my parents and grandparents

1

Anonsa was arranging her bags on the trolley at the baggage reclaim area in London Heathrow Airport, when she caught sight of a young man, who was staring fixedly at her.

'Who the hell is this man devouring me with his eyes so early in the morning?' Anonsa moaned quietly to herself.

Then something suddenly clicked in her brain and a wave of recognition flooded through her. The young man's name was Burnty Christopher and they were about the same age. She continued to arrange her bags. Burnty could not take his eyes off Anonsa, no matter how hard he tried. He had actually spotted her about thirty minutes earlier while she was getting off the plane. They had travelled on the same plane, a Boeing 747 from Lagos Airport in Nigeria.

Burnty already had his trolley loaded with his luggage: a bulging, large, black leather box and another greyish-coloured, suitcase. After dragging his eyes away from Anonsa, he left with his luggage hoping to wait for her in the arrivals lounge.

Burnty could still not remember precisely where he had met

1

this slim, tall, brown-complexioned beautiful woman, with the long eyelashes and well-manicured fingernails.

After waiting in the arrivals lounge for more than an hour, Burnty decided that he had to go on his way. He got up and tried to disentangle his jacket, which had accidentally caught on a piece of metal that projected from the trolley. He bent down to do this and as he straightened up, he saw Anonsa again. He walked confidently towards her. Anonsa stopped and smiled at him. This encouraged him to go further. So he said to her, 'Hello, I seem to know you from somewhere. You look very familiar.'

'You look familiar too,' responded Anonsa, stretching out her hand.

Burnty took her hand and shook it eagerly with a radiant smile on his face.

'Did you go to Romsey Memorial Grammar School in Ilorin?' asked Anonsa.

'Yes!' Burnty almost shouted.

Then suddenly he remembered everything. They had both been expelled from the school when they were in their second year.

'What's your name again?' queried Burnty.

'Anonsa Omiyale. And aren't you Burnty?' responded Anonsa.

She was not likely to forget the boy who had brought humiliation and near-ruin upon her all those years ago.

'Yes. I'm Burnty Christopher. But I thought you had a Yoruba name then?' Burnty said, still trying hard to remember it.

'Yes, you're right. My Yoruba name is Pelu, but I switched to Anonsa which is my middle name.' Anonsa chuckled to herself before she continued, 'Let's walk towards the taxi rank.'

Burnty fiddled with his red-striped tie.

While they were in High School, Burnty and Anonsa had been

caught together in the girls' toilet touching and kissing each other. They had thought there was nobody around until a student walked in and saw them through the open door. She was aghast and quickly ran out to report them to a member of staff. Mr Walag, on being told, immediately dashed into the toilets and found Burnty and Anonsa, who were still fondling each other without much seeming to care who was watching them.

'What do you think you are doing? Where do you think you are? In some cheap brothel?' shouted Mr Walag. 'Now both of you can march straight to the Principal's office.'

Burnty and Anonsa looked up and saw Mr Walag standing there with eyes blazing and arms folded across his chest. They nearly fainted with fear and amazement. They hastily buttoned up their clothes and were marched to the office of the school principal, Mr Gutu Regede. Mr Regede had a reputation for being a no-nonsense, firm, disciplinarian who was credited with having restored order to Romsey Memorial Grammar School, which had been notorious for its wayward students. On reaching Mr Regede's office, they were ordered to kneel down on the bare floor as the first stage of their punishment. Within minutes, many students had gathered outside the office to watch the scene and they had to be driven back to their classrooms by the school prefects. Burnty and Anonsa were weeping and shaking with fright, begging to be forgiven. They could already sense what was in store for them, knowing what had happened to other students who had committed lesser offences. After a few hours, Mr Regede arrived back from the meeting he had been attending in the State's Ministry of Education. As soon as he walked into his office, Mr Walag told him what had happened. Mr Regede flew into a rage and started shouting.

'How dare you try to ruin my school's reputation in such a sordid way? If you're already behaving like this at *your*, age, what will you be like in a few years' time? You will definitely not be allowed to remain here, setting a bad example for others. You will be hearing from me shortly. Now you can both get out of my office . . .'

Burnty's face was soaked with hot tears as he ran out of the office saying, 'Please sir, forgive us. Don't expel us.'

Anonsa, who at twelve was a year older than Burnty, was also crying and trying desperately to dry her tears. She did not utter a word. She merely walked out with her head bowed. While Mr Walag was summoned by Mr Regede, who listened attentively to the story in detail, Anonsa and Burnty were sent back to their classes.

On reaching home that day, Anonsa told her mother, Susan, what had happened. Her mother was a dental surgeon who ran a private practice in town. She was completely flattened by the news, despite the fact that she had raised Anonsa to be honest with her and tell her whenever she got into trouble. Susan began to mumble to herself, 'What did I do wrong? Anonsa, why did you do this to me . . . ?' She had been bringing her daughter up alone for the past six years, since her husband's death from throat cancer. Now she found herself questioning how good a job she was doing. Anonsa remained quiet as she always did whenever she got into trouble.

Burnty on the other hand, was afraid to tell his parents about what had happened. His father was a school teacher and as both his parents were devout Christians he had been brought up under a very strict religious code. So Burnty kept the secret to himself and, being the only one of seven siblings who attended Romsey Memorial Grammar School, none of his family knew that anything had happened, except that he had suddenly become quiet and withdrawn.

4

After a few days of taunting and name-calling from the other students, Burnty and Anonsa settled down again, until about three weeks later when they were suddenly summoned to Mr Regede's office. It was in the morning and the rain was falling heavily, when their class captain, Matola Lucas, suddenly announced, 'Burnty, the principal would like to see you now,' he continued, 'And you too Pelu.'

On hearing this, Burnty's heart skipped a beat and he began to breathe faster, sensing what probably awaited him. Anonsa's mother had already made arrangements for her to be sent to another school if she was expelled, so she was calm as she walked to the Principal's office.

'Sit down,' ordered Mr Regede, when they arrived. 'I have conducted a thorough investigation into what happened and have decided that you will both be expelled from this school with immediate effect.' He stood up and proceeded to give them official letters stating his decision. On hearing this, Burnty nearly fainted but Anonsa remained calm. They took their letters and walked out of Mr Regede's office, looking sober. Then both left the school immediately and headed to their respective homes.

Since that moment, they had never set eyes on each other, until now, when they met in Heathrow Airport.

The taxi that Burnty and Anonsa were sharing had left the airport and was now moving towards Great Portland Street.

'The office of the General Medical Council is on this street,' said Anonsa.

'Please don't tell me you are a doctor,' said Burnty.

'But I am. I'm about to start a new job as specialist registrar in public health in Swansea. How about you?'

'I am a dentist. I recently went for an interview for a specialist registrar's post in maxillofacial surgery in Glasgow. Isn't it marvellous that we have both gone into similar professions?'

Burnty was immensely pleased to know that Anonsa was now a doctor.

'But you haven't told me yet, why you dropped your name and changed it to Anonsa?'

'I didn't really *change* my name, I just started using my middle name instead, so that I wouldn't forever be known as Pelu – the girl who was expelled from Romsey.'

After being expelled, Anonsa's mother had sent her out of town to live with her Aunt Veronica, who was a lecturer in the Faculty of Law at the University of Jos. Anonsa had gone to the University of Jos Secondary School and then to the University itself, where she studied medicine for six years. After qualifying as a doctor, she completed her internship at the University's Teaching Hospital before coming to the UK for further studies. Having been born in London at Guy's Hospital Anonsa was already a British citizen.

After Burnty was expelled from the Romsey Memorial Grammar School, his parents had initially refused to help him as they thought he should be taught a lesson. Eventually he had been admitted to the Baptist Academy in Lagos and then studied dentistry at the university there.

After qualifying as a dentist, Burnty had done his internship training at the Lagos University Teaching Hospital and then completed his National Youth Service Corp assignment at the General Hospital in Yola, Adamawa State. Afterwards he had also travelled to the UK, for postgraduate dental training.

'Where are you going now?' queried Burnty.

'I'm heading home, which at the moment is in North London,

but next Tuesday I'll be moving to Swansea to start my new job. How about you?'

'I live in Leicester but I'll be staying in London tonight.'

'What's your phone number?'

Anonsa opened her handbag and got out a pen so they could exchange telephone numbers. When the taxi pulled up at her home, Anonsa promised to phone Burnty and said goodbye, leaving him to travel on alone to his destination in West London.

2

March 2004

'This food is not bad, although I'm not that hungry,' Anonsa said as she bit into a portion of the steak which she had been served.

'I agree with you. It's quite delicious. As for me my favourite food is always *amala* and *ewedu* soup, but since I arrived in the UK, I have learnt to enjoy the various kinds of food in the restaurants where I normally eat,' said Burnty.

'Do you need anything, sir?' asked one of the waiters who passed by their table.

'No, thank you,' said Burnty.

They were at the Bardinott Restaurant on Charing Cross Road, where they were dining out for the second time since their chance meeting in Heathrow Airport two months earlier. The owner of the restaurant was called Tanru, and he was Italian. He had been running the restaurant for over ten years and liked to regale his customers with stories of how he came to London with little money and set up the restaurant by dint of sheer hard work.

The Bardinott was a popular spot for medics. They liked to

dine there whenever they were in London, especially those who lived outside the city. How this came about was unclear, though rumour had it that a few years previously the British Medical Association had hosted a dinner at the Bardinott which was very successful. The restaurant was well-liked by those who had attended and the news quickly spread by word of mouth to other doctors and dentists.

'How are you finding your new job in Swansea? I guess you must have more responsibilities by now.'

'As a matter of fact, I am really enjoying the job. I have plenty of time on my hands after work too, ever since I broke up with my boyfriend.'

Being a smart lady and a wily seductress, she was trying to test the waters to find out whether Burnty was engaged. She knew that he wasn't married yet. She was able to pick up that piece of information during their last meeting in the same restaurant. They had both been cautious about delving into emotional matters ever since their first meeting in London.

Burnty was a bit nervous; not knowing how to respond. He had promised himself not to go near emotional issues, at least for now. He felt that it was too early to do so. Moreover, he did not want to look vulnerable, having recently broken up with his girlfriend of three years which had left him completely shattered.

His girlfriend, Emily Braithwaite, had left him for another man who was divorced. They had first met at the Lagos University Teaching Hospital, when Emily was a medical student on an elective posting in Nigeria. She was British, white and came from Northampton. She had graduated in medicine from the University of Leicester. After Emily finished her elective posting in Nigeria and returned to the UK they didn't see each other again until one day they suddenly met in Leicester, where they were both working, and rekindled their relationship from there.

'I am trying to enjoy my own job. You know, it gets really boring when you keep doing the same senior house officer job, which they sometimes glorify as a clinical research fellow. I feel that I'm long overdue for a specialist registrar job. But I am making the best of it at the moment. What else can I do after all?'

Burnty sounded despondent.

'Burnty, pardon me for asking, but do you have a girlfriend? Otherwise, what do you do in your spare time?'

Anonsa was very direct.

The questions hit Burnty like a thunderbolt. Not knowing what to say, he began to stammer, 'Eh ... eh ... well, I had a girl-friend. I thought we were going to get married but unfortunately we broke up with each other recently.'

Anonsa heaved a sigh of relief. Her feelings for Burnty seemed to have rekindled, which surprised her, as it wasn't that long since they'd met again. Burnty definitely still found her attractive now that they'd both developed into full-grown adults, but he had been frightened of showing it.

'I'm sorry about that.'

'Thank you.'

'You look quite fit. Are you into sports?'

Anonsa tried to change the subject now that she had found out what she wanted to know.

'Yes. I do a lot of exercise in the gym and I also play squash, cricket and tennis.'

'That's interesting. I love watching tennis, even though I don't play it. Have you been following the tennis grand slam champion-ships recently?'

'Do you mean Wimbledon, the US, French and Australian Opens?'

'Yes.'

'There was a young man from Switzerland who was domi-
nating the Men's Singles event. He is very talented, but I can't
seem to be able to recall his name. It's something Federer . . .'

'Do you mean Roger Federer?' Anonsa cut in.

'Yes, that's him!' Burnty said enthusiastically, 'And the Williams
sisters still seem to be doing well. I am particularly fascinated by
a young British teenager who played well in the last Wimbledon
Championship.'

'That must be Andrew Murray from Scotland you're talking
about,' Anonsa was trying to impress him with her up-to-date
knowledge of tennis.

'You seem to know a lot about tennis, even though you don't
play the game,' Burnty flattered her.

'Well, it's just one of those things.'

Anonsa tried to make little of the compliment even though
she was secretly filled with delight.

'How about your family in Nigeria?'

'Oh, I lost my dad a very long time ago. He died of throat
cancer when I was very young. My mum is still in private dental
practice in Ilorin, though she travels very frequently to see me in
the UK. My twin younger brothers are in America and they are
both lawyers, they both graduated from Harvard. One of them
practises in New York while the other is based in Raleigh, North
Carolina. They are both married, each with two kids.'

'How about here in the UK?'

'I have many relatives here and we see each other and speak
to each other from time to time. How about you?'

'I never really realised, when we were at school together, that
your father was dead. I'm sorry about that. My parents are in
Nigeria and they are both elderly now. My older siblings are

11

married. Some of them live in Nigeria while some live in Canada. My younger brother, Robert, who studied medicine at the University of Ibadan is now doing his residency training in internal medicine at Johns Hopkins University Hospital, in Baltimore. Here in the UK I also have quite a few relatives.'

'It's hard to keep in touch with everybody these days, we're all so busy.'

'That's quite true. I agree with you. I am really delighted to see you again after all these years. I believe it's the hand of destiny at work. I could never have imagined that I would see you again. I hope something good comes out of it.'

Burnty smiled. 'I hope so too.'

Anonsa was searching for her purse which was inside her brown, Gucci handbag. She had insisted from the outset that she would pay for dinner this time, as Burnty had paid on their previous outing. He allowed her to have her way and she was pleased about this.

'I like this handbag of yours, you are always so well turned out,' Burnty complimented her.

'What else can we women do if we want you to look at us?'

They both burst into laughter. After she had settled the bill, leaving a generous tip, they got up from their seats and began to walk out of the restaurant.

'You are very generous to the waiters with your tips. Many of them come from all over the world and they are always impeccably dressed and well-mannered. I really like the international atmosphere here.'

'That's one of the reasons why I like to dine here myself.'

They walked out of the restaurant, holding each other's hands and laughing.

3

November 2003

'Oh my goodness!' shouted Burnty, 'I am late for duty now. What's going on? I rarely wake up so late.'

He began to prowl from one end of the veranda to the other, then suddenly he stopped and began to cry as he thought about Emily, his ex-girlfriend, who had left him for another man.

Very few people who had known them when they were together would have believed that they could break up, they seemed so happy together. They had bought a house together in Leicester, where they both lived and worked and had even broached the subject of getting engaged when disaster struck. It all started when Emily went shopping at Tesco one weekend, when Burnty was on-call at the hospital. She was driving into the car park, when suddenly a grey VW Golf being driven by a white man in his late forties veered towards her. Emily was shaken by this near-collision and when they both got out of their cars, the man walked up to her and apologized profusely.

He said, 'I'm so sorry about that, I hope you're not too upset?'

'No, thank you,' Emily smiled.

'My name is Richard.'

'I'm Emily.'

Emily looked a bit embarrassed but she was polite. After the man had made sure she was alright, he left. Emily went into Tesco and did her shopping, then drove back home to prepare lunch for Burnty, who always liked to come home to eat at the weekend even when he was on duty.

Emily had all but forgotten about this incident and she didn't even bother to mention it to Burnty. Then, a few months later, Emily went to renew the MOT on her car in one of the garages in Leicester while Burnty was travelling to Nigeria, and she met the man again, instantly recognizing him. Richard was of average build and height and he looked quite athletic. He had also instantly recognized Emily and began to walk towards her when he suddenly tripped and fell when one of the mechanics inadvertently bumped into him. Before Richard could get up, Emily was by his side and he stood up to see her standing directly in front of him.

'Oh dear, I'm sorry. Are you OK? You do look familiar. Are you Richard?' asked Emily.

'Yes, I am and thank you. I was actually walking towards you to find out if you were the woman I nearly drove into at Tesco a few months ago, when I tripped. You're Emily, aren't you?'

'You are quite right. How are you? I'm here for an MOT.'

Emily put her car keys into her handbag. She was pleased that she was not looking as shabby as she usually did when she rushed to the garage to have her car serviced.

'I'm alright, thank you.'

'You look great,' said Richard, trying to compliment her.

'Oh, thank you,' replied Emily matter-of-factly.

She was the reticent type, though quite capable of making long speeches when the occasion called for it.

'Would you like to join me for coffee when your MOT is done?'

'That would be nice, thank you.'

Emily had a vague smile on her face. She had been feeling lonely since Burnty left for Nigeria the week before to visit his mother, who was suddenly taken ill. Even though Burnty phoned her every day, she sometimes felt a bit low emotionally. Her parents were both divorced and had remarried, but they still often phoned her to see how she was doing, especially her mother. Her two younger sisters were both married and the youngest, Lala, was a successful actress in Hollywood. Her other sister, Helen, lived in Truro with her husband who was often away on business. Helen was a full-time housewife, having resigned from her job as a Spanish and Japanese translator. Sometimes Emily went to see her, but she hadn't felt like it this weekend.

About an hour later, Emily and Richard were sitting together round a table in the nearby Caffè Nero, drinking black coffee.

'Thanks for saying that I looked nice earlier. You look good yourself.'

Emily was trying to start a discussion.

'That's very kind of you. Thank you,' he responded shyly.

Richard, who began to fiddle with his shirt buttons, had never been comfortable with compliments. His father was an easy-going man who never laid his hands on his children but starved them of love and affection. Richard's mother, who was a dancer in a Theatre Company, had left his father for another man when Richard was ten years old and he grew up with his father. The man had never remarried, he had single-handedly raised Richard and his elder brother Matthew. Richard's upbringing might have been bereft of affection but he did not lack materially. He went to Eton College and Bristol University where he studied business and politics. On graduation he formed his own company running a string of Fitness Centres in Leicester, Leeds and Bradford. He got married at the age of twenty-eight to the daughter of a wealthy British businessman who was based in Bangkok. They had two children, a boy and a girl, and were happy together until he found out that his wife was cheating on him with another woman. They had divorced and both kids now lived with their mother in Surrey.

'Do you live in town?' enquired Richard.

'Yes I do.'

'Are you married?'

'No, but I live with my boyfriend who is a dentist from Nigeria. He's over there at the moment seeing his mum who has been ill. We're very happy together.'

Emily was trying to ward off any advances, so she deliberately did not ask him whether or not he was married.

'That's nice to know. As for me, I'm divorced from my wife of over thirteen years and we have two kids. If you don't mind my asking you, what do you do for a living?'

'I'm a doctor in postgraduate training in paediatrics at the Royal Infirmary, which is part of the University Hospital Leicester NHS Trust.'

'Hm, that's interesting. You must be very clever.'

'Well, thank you,' Emily blushed.

Richard had always been in awe of medics; his older brother had wanted to study medicine but his A Level results had not been good enough.

'How about you?' Emily summoned up the courage to ask him. Even though initially she hadn't wanted to give him the slightest indication that she might be interested in him, she was now enjoying the discussion.

'I run a Fitness Centre in town.'

'That's interesting.'

Their coffee cups were now empty so they got up to leave after Richard had paid for their drinks.

'Thank you,' said Emily.

'It's my pleasure. I hope to see you again some time,' said Richard, before they parted.

That evening, Emily went to the De Grate nightclub with her friend Natasha. While she was on the dance floor, she spotted Richard who was also dancing in the far corner of the room. She was surprised to see him again so soon and began to get paranoid and wonder whether Richard was following her. So she continued dancing and pretended not to have seen him. Richard didn't even notice her and after a few hours Emily accepted that she was not being tailed by him and that his presence there was just a coincidence. She began to be annoyed that Richard had not spotted her and kept casting furtive glances in his direction, hoping that their eyes would meet. She was quite drunk and struggled to stay standing as she danced. When she looked round again she couldn't see Richard on the dance floor; and she gave up on him. Natasha was not someone who liked to dance for hours, so after a while she suggested to Emily that they should go home. As they came out of the club together, holding each other's arms, Emily saw Richard standing by the taxi rank with a friend. He was speaking to one of the taxi drivers when he turned and saw Emily waving at him. He was thrilled to see her again as he had found it very difficult to take his mind off her since they parted earlier in the day at the café. He was smitten with her, and here she was again – the object of his massive crush.

He staggered and said, 'Hi Emily. It's wonderful to see you again so soon. Don't tell me that you've been at the De Grate!'

'It's lovely to see you too. Yes, we've been at the De Grate, it's my favourite nightclub in Leicester,' Emily replied. She didn't

17

mention the fact that she had actually spotted him in the club, her ego prevented her from admitting that.

'Where are you going now?' queried Richard.

'Home,' said Emily.

'Would you like to see my new house? It's just around the corner. I had a house-warming party just two months ago.'

'That's a nice idea,' said Emily.

She would not have agreed to this suggestion had she been sober, but she wasn't, and Natasha was quick to go along with it as she already had her eyes on Richard's friend, Bruce. All four of them got into the taxi. Richard sat in front with the driver while the others bundled into the back seat, with Natasha in the middle. Emily and Richard made the necessary introductions.

'Can you stop here please?' Richard asked the driver.

After the driver had parked in front of Richard's house, all four of them got out and Richard paid the fare.

'Richard, you've got a lovely house here,' said Natasha.

'Thank you. My home is my castle, as the saying goes,' said Richard, who was delighted by the compliment.

Richard opened the front door and led his guests into the living room. He told them to make themselves comfortable on the sofas, then went into the kitchen to get them some drinks.

'It's nice to meet you both,' Bruce said, 'Do you both live in Leicester?'

'Yes,' said Emily and Natasha almost simultaneously.

Emily was now lying on the sofa, she was almost falling asleep. Natasha was a bit more sober and she continued to chat with Bruce.

'Emily, are you alright?' queried Natasha.

'Yes, I am. I'm just feeling a bit tired,' said Emily.

'Do you live in Leicester too?' Natasha asked Bruce.

'Yes. I work for a computer firm as a manager,' said Bruce.

'That's interesting . . .' said Natasha before she was cut short by Richard's entry into the living room. It was past midnight.

'I hope you are all comfortable?' Richard said. 'Would you ladies like a tour of the house? Bruce has been here several times already.'

Richard led Emily and Natasha through the house until eventually they reached the bedroom. He then showed them a framed photograph of himself with his ex-wife and their two children.

'How lovely you all look there together,' said Emily.

'We were a very close family until the divorce.'

Emily was overwhelmed by the atmosphere of togetherness in the picture. It reminded her of her own childhood when her parents were always fighting and never seemed to be able to agree on anything. She felt vulnerable and in need of love. Then, suddenly, she hugged Richard and they both collapsed onto the bed. Richard pretended to be startled, but he was actually enjoying it and feeling really aroused. He bent over her and said, 'Are you alright, Emily?'

'Yes. I'm just very tired and I don't think I can go home now,' said Emily.

Natasha was quiet and did not know what to say. She had known Emily since they were in high school together and had seen her friend behave very strangely before when she was interested in a man.

Richard leant over Emily and kissed her on the cheeks. He kept on asking her 'Are you alright?'

As Natasha made to leave the room, clearly embarrassed by the spectacle and also slightly jealous, Bruce came into the bedroom. He held Natasha's hand and they went to the adjoining bedroom together. 'If you feel you can't go home, you're very welcome to stay overnight,' said Richard.

By now they were both kissing each other passionately. Emily was lying in bed topless after pulling off her dress and was fiddling with the zip on Richard's trousers. Richard's hands caressed her full breasts tenderly. Emily reached for his penis which was bulging through his underpants and within minutes he was inside her. He thrust hard and fast while she screamed in delight. Meanwhile, Bruce and Natasha were also making love in the adjoining bedroom.

'Hey! It's 5.00 a.m. I have to go home now,' said Emily. She and Richard had both fallen asleep after their exhausting lovemaking on the previous night.

'Won't you have breakfast before you go?'

Richard's arms were wrapped round her and they smiled at each other.

'No, I have to get home, just in case Burnty phones.'

Natasha and Bruce were still soundly asleep in their room.

4

'Goodbye dad, I'll soon be going to the train station to meet Burnty. He's returning from Nigeria today,' said Emily.

'Goodbye honey, I'll speak to you soon,' came the voice from the other end of the phone.

Emily's father, Nathaniel, had rung up to speak to her, after many months. Emily was delighted to hear from him again even though she had been reluctant to call him. She had been upset because her father had not phoned back after she called him about four months previously and she hadn't been able to reach him at home, at work, or even on his cell phone.

'It was nice to speak to daddy again, after all this time,' Emily said to herself as she got ready to drive to the station to collect Burnty.

'We all need to be surrounded by the love of people who are close to us especially our parents, siblings and even extended family and friends,' Emily mused. 'No one should be deprived of such love for any reason, because it is anathema to our human nature. I'm in a better mood now, so I can happily drive to pick up Burnty.'

21

Emily went outside to get into her car. '*Oops!*' exclaimed Emily at the sight of her car windscreen, which was completely covered by ice. 'I should have put the car away in the garage last night'

'*What foul weather we have today,*' she said to herself as she sprayed de-icer on her windows. She then switched on the engine and waited for the windscreen to clear, listening to the radio while she sat there.

'*Today's weather is better, no delays anywhere on the roads . . .*' came the news over the radio.

'Thank goodness,' said Emily to herself. She had been anxious about the traffic situation because the city had witnessed a serious logjam and diversions in the previous two days. As soon as she was able to see clearly through the windscreen Emily drove off towards the train station. The traffic on the road was relatively light compared to what she was used to and, being a Sunday, she was hoping they would be able to get to the 3.00 p.m. service at Saint Nicholas Church in the city.

The trees which lined the roads were swaying in the wind. A group of people of all ages, carrying backpacks, was gathered at one of the road junctions close to the Royal Infirmary and they were being addressed by a short, middle-aged man. He was wearing a dark green jacket with 'tour guide' written on the back. He was still talking to the tourists and pointing at different buildings as they all started to move along the road.

Emily began to think about her recent conversation with her father. She had not expected the call and had only just woken up when the phone rang. She had initially thought that it must be Burnty who was phoning, only for her father's voice to boom down the receiver saying, 'How are you honey?' – which was how he liked to address her. Emily had been completely nonplussed. She did not know whether to cry or laugh and all her grudges just melted away instantly. Her father had always been reluctant to phone her too frequently, believing, wrongly, that he needed to give her some space now she was an adult with a life of her own. But that's not what Emily wanted. She had never really recovered from the trauma of her parents' separation and eventual divorce and she had always craved a lot of attention from them both. Ever since her father remarried and moved with his wife to Australia, she had consistently turned down his invitations to visit them. She found it difficult to accept his new wife because she was too jealous of the new woman in his life. This had been the situation for over ten years now and Emily had only just agreed to visit her father in Sydney, where he lived with his wife and two adopted sons. Emily was now desperate to meet her step-brothers knowing that she might become a mother herself in the future, as her two younger sisters had.

'You can never trust these radio announcements,' Emily muttered as she saw a line of stationary vehicles in front of her and a group of policemen diverting the traffic. The area was cordoned off. Emily wondered why, until she drove past and saw that a black jeep had collided with a tree.

Emily's cell phone rang and she quickly snapped it open and answered briskly. 'I'm driving, I'm on my way. See you soon,' she said and she switched off the phone. It was Burnty who had rung her, to say that he had now arrived at the station.

'Hi darling, sweetie, my ever gorgeous heartthrob,' shouted Burnty as soon as he caught sight of Emily, who was parking her car in the car park. Emily, however, had not seen him as she was still deciding where to park. She got out of the car, shut the door, and turned right towards the station building. Emily was wearing a smart, striped black suit with a pair of red, shoes. Her make-up was minimal and she wore the Cartier diamond-encrusted wrist watch which Burnty had bought her for her last birthday. She had had her hair cut into a bob and looked very attractive. 'I know that Burnty will like my outfit,' she muttered to herself.

As she turned round to cross the nearby road to walk towards the station waiting room, she saw Burnty running towards her empty handed.

'Hi darling. It's so nice to see you. I'm glad they didn't change your flight schedule. I thank God that you are back,' said Emily as she hugged Burnty, who was breathless from running to get to her. They kissed each other passionately and looked delighted to be together again.

'Thank you, darling. I'm thrilled to be back.'

'How's your mum?' enquired Emily.

Burnty had spared her the heart-rending details of his mother's hospitalization each time they had spoken over the phone, knowing that Emily was not very good at hearing about the sufferings of people who were close to her, even though she was a doctor herself.

'Mum's condition is now stable but she is still on the surgical ward at the Lagos University Teaching Hospital, convalescing,' said Burnty. They held hands and began to walk towards the waiting room to collect Burnty's luggage, which he had left temporarily in the care of an elderly couple who were waiting to board a train.

'Which of the surgical wards is she in? Is it the one close to the gate leading to Mushin?' enquired Emily, who had shadowed doctors at the hospital briefly while she was a medical student.

'No. It's the one close to the gate leading to Surulere,' said Burnty as they finally arrived at the waiting room. He collected his luggage, after thanking the elderly couple for looking after it.

'Oh, I see. I'm happy to hear that. It's always tough when a parent is hospitalized. Even though my parents were divorced when I was young, I remember how anxious I was when my mum had a medical check-up in Germany, five years ago,' said Emily as she helped Burnty with his luggage.

'Mind your back. I don't want you to develop a slipped disc,' teased Burnty.

'Thank you and I know that you'll sort it out. How nice even to have the opportunity to tell the world that I got a slipped disc from carrying my boyfriend's bag. What better monument to love can there be? That'll be my own Taj Mahal,' responded Emily and both of them laughed as they jointly wheeled the trolley to the parked car.

About ten minutes later they were on the road approaching King's Street which led to their house.

'There don't seem to be many tourists this year,' said Burnty as Emily stopped at a red light.

'I saw lots of them when I was coming to the station earlier on today. They were with a very short man, who was their tour guide,' said Emily as the traffic light changed.

'How short was he?'

'Probably about 5 foot 3.'

'That's about my mum's height you know,' said Burnty. 'She really loved it because she used to stand out in a crowd and she got easily recognized, and she used to get plenty of positive attention as a result of that.'

'I don't think that someone's height should be such a big issue. People stare at very tall or very short people which often makes them uncomfortable and self-conscious. I remember a former classmate of mine at High School who was almost 6 foot 4 at the age of fifteen. She never felt comfortable, but luckily she won a scholarship to study Physical Education at UCLA in California and she now plays in the NBA League. She eventually reached a height of 6 foot 7 and she married a 7-foot tall, Hispanic-American who also played basketball.'

They were now in front of their house and Emily manoeuvred the car towards the garage.

'What a perfect match. We live in a world of very close scrutiny that has little tolerance for apparent exterior incompatibilities but tends to forget about internal similarities.'

'It's an amazing world.'

'I'm happy to be home,' said Burnty as he hugged Emily again. They kissed before opening the door to their house.

'So am I.'

On entering the house, Burnty collapsed onto the sofa in the sitting room. He saw a stack of mail which had arrived during his absence, lying on the centre table. It had been neatly arranged by Emily.

'I know that you are intending to go to church. I'll have to rest for a while before I start getting ready to go,' said Burnty.

'Of course, darling. I know that if I hadn't dressed up already you might find an excuse not to go to church today,' said Emily giggling.

'Would this be your usual theocratic pressure?' joked Burnty and they started laughing. He went upstairs to change.

It was the weekend and the fourth day of Emily and Burnty's annual leave, a week after Burnty's return from Nigeria. He had been given emergency leave from work to enable him travel to see his mother before the start of his annual leave.

Emily and Burnty were still lying huddled together in bed beneath the sheets after a night of passionate lovemaking. They were awake and Emily was stroking the hairs on Burnty's chest while he touched and stroked her breasts tenderly. A Rolling Stones track was blaring out from the CD player lying on the nearby table.

'Switch on the TV please,' Burnty asked.

Emily reached for the remote control.

'How much are you going to pay? Bear in mind it's pay per view,' joked Emily as she switched on the TV and tuned in to Sky News.

'Good morning, this is Sky World news,' the broadcaster said. 'The United Nations is to celebrate its Anniversary today in New York and many world leaders are expected to attend . . .'

'It's the UN again,' cut in Emily. 'There was a news item yesterday about the World Health Organization's activities and now it's a celebration of an anniversary.'

'The UN has many divisions: WHO, IMF, UNESCO, UNICEF, and so on and so forth and each organization is independent of the others. I think it is worth celebrating an organization that has helped to maintain world peace since the devastation caused by the Second World War,' said Burnty. 'Over seventy million people were said to have lost their lives during the Second World War and I believe that the entire human race would not want a repetition of such a disaster again.'

'I hope you are not trying to topple the current Secretary-General of the UN? Please let him finish his tenure because with your present eloquence and knowledge about UN activities, you may be in line for the post of the UN Secretary-General,' teased Emily who was now sitting up in bed.

'And what would you be called? Madam Secretary-General or UN First Lady?'

They both burst out laughing.

27

'Seriously though, I think I agree with you,' began Emily. 'But what about all the other war going on in many parts of the world?'

'Don't you support the idea of having an organization like the UN?'

'Of course I do. Maybe we should take our debate to the London School of Economics and Political Science as a guest couple . . .'

They were interrupted by a loud thump that came from the study. It was as if something had dropped onto the floor.

'Darling, let me check quickly. I have a feeling that the books have fallen off the bookshelf,' said Burnty as he jumped out of bed. He put on his dressing gown and walked to the study, where he found several books lying scattered on the floor.

'I thought as much,' he said, as he began to pick them up.

'What was it?' shouted Emily from the bedroom.

'It's the books. I'm arranging them back on the shelf,' responded Burnty.

Back in the bedroom, Burnty sat on the edge of the bed while Emily watched a programme on Channel Four.

'We said that we'd join Astrid and Nigel at the Salamander Restaurant at two o'clock, so I'd better get some clothes on,' said Emily as she got out of bed.

'That's true.'

'One of those Operative Surgery textbooks of yours is still lying on the floor, I thought you had put all the books back,' said Emily as she peeped into the study on the way past.

'I'll sort it out later.'

'What's for breakfast?'

'Guess?'

'The usual scrambled eggs on toast with sausage and baked

beans, and your trademark tea. Or do you want something else?' said Emily coquettishly.

'No. We had that last night!'

'Fine.'

They both started laughing.

'What about Nigel and Astrid's daughter? I hope they are bringing her along.'

'Yes, they are. She's seven now and is attending a special school that caters to the needs of gifted children. Her parents initially thought that she was slow because she was having problems at school. It was only after they had a meeting with the school authorities that they found out she has a mental age of fifteen and would therefore need to be transferred to another school, where her needs could be met.'

'Really?' Burnty looked thoroughly amazed. 'I haven't met her yet.'

'She is a lovely, quick-witted girl and is very well behaved.'

Astrid had been Emily's classmate at High School and they were close friends. Astrid's parents had also divorced but four years later they got married again. Her parents and Emily's parents used to meet at parent evenings and they swapped stories of how difficult it was to be divorced.

Astrid was amongst the brightest students in her class and could also dance, sing and act. Everyone at school thought she would go on to become an actress.

She was born in Britain but her father was Italian and her mother was from Honduras and they had settled in Britain twenty years before she was born. She met her husband, Nigel, through a mutual friend.

Nigel was born in Aberdeen but grew up in England. His parents were both English and he worked as a partner in a firm of chartered accountants in London, where he and Astrid lived.

Nigel's parents lived in Leicester and it was while he and Astrid were visiting them, that they ran into Emily, at the The Shires Shopping Centre. Emily and Astrid hadn't seen each other since they left school. There was near pandemonium among the crowd, when they rushed to embrace each other. They had been so excited to see each other again that Nigel had watched with a tinge of jealousy and looked a little lonely as they hugged each other. They exchanged phone numbers and promised to get in touch. The promise was kept, and Astrid phoned Emily one after-noon while she was at work in the hospital and they agreed to meet at the Salamander Restaurant the next time Astrid and Nigel were visiting Leicester.

Burnty cleared the table after they had eaten breakfast, while Emily went to fix her hair.

Burnty was behind the wheel as they arrived at the Salamander Restaurant, an Italian place with a reputation for smartly dressed and courteous staff. He parked nearby and they arrived outside the restaurant just before two o'clock. Nigel, Astrid and their daughter, Chloe, were already seated at the table which they had booked.

'Hello Astrid,' said Emily as they hugged each other. 'This is my partner, Burnty. I've already met Nigel and Chloe before.'

'Good afternoon. I'm Burnty,' said Burnty while he shook hands with Nigel and Astrid. 'How are you Chloe?'

'I'm fine, thank you,' said Chloe.

Burnty then took his seat beside Emily.

'I hope you haven't been waiting for too long?' Emily said.

'No, thank you. We only arrived a few minutes ago. We were a bit early and you weren't late, if anything I think you are both early too,' responded Astrid as they all smiled. A waitress courteously stood by waiting to take orders, so they all began to go through the menu.

'What's been happening to you, Astrid?' asked Emily.

'We haven't really had time to catch up properly on the phone,' said Astrid. 'After I left Cambridge, I went to work with the World Bank for five years before joining Deutsche Bank in London.'

'World Bank? It must have been exciting there I suppose?' said Emily.

'I was based in Copenhagen where the World Bank had a project going on at the time. Sometimes I also travelled to Oslo and Helsinki for short periods of time,' said Astrid, while the men looked on with interest.

'You must speak some Danish then,' said Emily.

'Unfortunately not very much. I only have a smattering of Danish – phrases like "*hvordan har du det*," which means "how are you?" and a few other words. It was when I came to London that I met Nigel,' said Astrid. 'What about you, Emily?'

'I went to Leicester to study and since qualifying I've worked in the Leicester area at different hospitals. I actually first met Burnty in Nigeria, while I was doing my elective in Lagos and then again at the Royal Infirmary, where we both work now,' Emily said. The waitress began to bring their food to the table.

'The men are keeping very quiet,' joked Emily.

'They are gallant gentlemen, allowing the ladies to go first before taking over,' said Astrid and they all laughed together.

'I went to University in Durham to study accounting and later joined a firm of chartered accountants in London, where I'm now a partner,' said Nigel.

'I trained as a dentist in Nigeria at the University of Lagos and I later came over to the UK after graduation to do my post-graduate training,' Burnty said.

31

'It must be a long way. Do you miss home?' said Nigel.

'Well, I'm used to it now. I've been living here for more than five years and with Emily by my side, I don't miss home. My home is here, now, with Emily,' said Burnty. He looked at Emily and they both smiled at each other as their eyes met.

'Have you ever been to Africa?' asked Burnty.

'Yes. I've been to Tanzania, but that was a very long time ago. It was during my gap year after I finished my A Levels. I remember we were originally supposed to go to Botswana but, unfortunately, a crisis broke out there that warranted a change to Tanzania. I was only there for a few months but, I thoroughly enjoyed the experience. But that's about the only place I've been to in Africa,' said Nigel. 'Astrid has travelled to more places than I have.'

'Not really. I've been to Ghana, Lesotho, Kenya, Cameroon and Angola. I narrowly missed going to Nigeria. The World Bank project which was going on in Zaria at the time had just finished when I joined them and I was sent to Copenhagen instead,' said Astrid.

'That's interesting,' said Burnty. 'I have only been to a few African countries myself even though I'm from Africa.'

A waiter then came over to the table to take orders for more drinks and Nigel ordered more orange juice for himself and Chloe. As they continued eating, CNN was showing a clip of the wedding ceremony between Anita Schofield, an American model and Bernard Bamsfield, a Hollywood actor, which took place in Prague.

'This is very interesting. My parents were married in Prague,' said Astrid, who was sipping red wine. 'My mother was working as a model too when she met and married my dad before she went into acting. But that's where the similarities end, my dad was not an actor, he was a landscape gardener. This is just fabulous.'

'I remember that you were really good at acting and everyone thought that you would end up as an actress. I still remember the role of "Agatha" which you played so well, but I can't remember the title of the play,' said Emily.

'Was it *Never Say Fail?*' said Astrid.

'Yes! That was the name. It's amazing that you still remember,' said Emily.

'It's easier to remember when you were directly involved,' said Astrid. 'Did you tell me back then that one of your sisters wanted to become an actress?'

'Yes, that's right! It's astonishing that you can still recollect all these things after such a long time. Lala made it into acting eventually and she now lives in Hollywood with her husband who's also an actor. But she did encounter some difficulties initially because my parents were not supportive of her choice of career. She insisted that that was what she wanted to do and my parents eventually gave in when they found out that she was very talented and was sought after by big time film directors. She even came close to getting a role in the Bond movie *Live and Let Die* but she was turned down at the last minute when they found someone they thought was more suitable for the role,' said Emily.

'That's interesting. Before my mum retired from acting a few years ago, she was in over sixty movies,' said Astrid.

'Why did she retire?' queried Emily.

'She was diagnosed with scleroderma which became so crippling that her doctors advised her to quit acting. She is still very passionate about modelling and acting. She spent five years modelling for a number of fashion houses before becoming an actress. She was the one who suggested the name, Chloe, for our daughter, as a tribute to her modelling career and Nigel and I accepted it,' said Astrid, while Nigel began to smile.

'I think it's a gorgeous name and as soon as Astrid mentioned it I instantly fell in love with the name and Chloe loves it too,' cut in Nigel.

Chloe looked on with delight and she said, 'Yes, daddy, I really love my name because there's no one else with the same name in my school and I get noticed very quickly by my teachers because of that.'

'Burnty, what's acting like in Nigeria?' asked Astrid.

'When I was growing up in Nigeria, it was not very popular because there was no big market for it then. The situation has changed now but you can't still compare it to the industry in the West, especially Hollywood, in terms of its lucrativeness. The same thing applied to modelling until the M-Net Face of Africa competition was won by a young Nigerian girl at the time,' said Burnty.

'Was it Oluchi Onweagba?' said Astrid.

'Yes that's right. You seem to know a lot about these things,' said Burnty, as he passed Emily's empty plate to the waiter who was clearing their table.

'It's because my mum subscribed to many fashion magazines, some of which she used to send to me,' said Astrid.

'Mummy, have you told them that I want them to come to my swimming competition?' asked Chloe.

'You must be a good swimmer if you're in a competition. Where does it take place?' asked Burnty.

'It's at the Fairies Fitness Club on Burley's Way and it's on a Saturday,' said Nigel and Astrid simultaneously.

Emily and Burnty began to flip through their diaries.

'I think Burnty and I can make it. Luckily neither of us has on-call commitments that day,' said Emily as she glanced at Burnty and they both smiled at each other.

'Thank you. I'm so happy now,' said Chloe and she began to jump up before her parents could thank Emily and Burnty for accepting the invitation.

They were now all on their feet, having settled the bill, and they agreed to meet again in the evening at the exclusive Blueshaft Nightclub. As they were leaving, Nigel began to feel in his pocket for his wallet when a young White man rushed into the restaurant with an empty beer bottle and smashed it over the head of the security guard who was standing by reception. There was instant confusion. Everyone rushed towards the door, the assailant was restrained and bundled out of the restaurant and the police were called. Luckily for the security guard, he was unhurt. Emily and the others were safely out of the restaurant and had quickened their pace when they heard someone shouting and running towards them. They all looked backwards but they could not make out who it was until the man got closer to them. It was one of the waiters, who had brought Nigel's wallet to him, which had mistakenly been left behind in their rush to get out of the restaurant.

Nigel thanked him and took the wallet. The waiter told them that the man who had assaulted the security guard had been to the restaurant earlier in the day begging for cigarettes. He was said to be notorious in the area for such behaviour and had received numerous cautions from the police in the past.

'That reminds me of Ethel who joined the Metropolitan Police after her A Levels,' said Emily.

'Do you mean that girl who used to read the detective novels? I'm not surprised, she was always interested in things like that, but I didn't realize she would join so quickly. I thought that she would wait until leaving University,' said Astrid, as they all walked along.

'That was her original plan, but she decided to join early when she started dating a young police officer while she was doing her A Levels. The officer had just left Nottingham University then and he encouraged her to join early,' said Emily.

'I wish her good luck. It must be a busy job, I guess,' said Astrid, before Nigel interrupted her.

'I'm so forgetful. Astrid, do you remember how I also left my wallet behind the other day at that restaurant close to your old office in Pimlico? It was never found. I wish I could just put it under my skin. I think medics called it "subcutaneous,"' said Nigel and he began to laugh.

'If wishes were horses, beggars would ride,' said Astrid.

'Emily, don't you think that it would be a wonderful break-through, if wallets could be implanted subcutaneously and retrieved at will as suggested by Nigel?' said Burnty, and all four of them laughed together.

'Mummy, why are you all laughing?' queried Chloe who looked on in amazement, not being able to understand what had been said.

'It's just a joke, Chloe,' said Astrid.

They finally said goodbye, promising to meet later that evening at the nightclub.

5

February 2003

Emily and Burnty's trip to the exclusive Blueshaft Nightclub was uneventful. They arrived twenty minutes early as they wanted to beat Astrid and Nigel this time around. Emily was dressed in a pair of smart red trousers with a matching jacket. She wore minimal make-up but had long artificial nails which were painted with bright red nail varnish.

Burnty was wearing a pair of dark brown trousers and a blue blazer over a light blue, long-sleeved shirt with gold cuff links.

As they were walking into the nightclub a black cab pulled up on the opposite side of the road and a man and woman emerged from inside. Emily stopped in her tracks and pulled Burnty backwards. 'Wait, it looks as though Astrid and Nigel have arrived,' she said.

'Are you sure it's them?' said Burnty.

As they watched the cab speed off, they found to their mutual amusement that the people were not in fact Astrid and Nigel. As the couple crossed the road and walked in the opposite direction, Burnty and Emily burst out laughing. They then went into the bar of the nightclub and ordered drinks for themselves. As they collected their drinks and looked around to find somewhere to sit, Astrid and Nigel entered the bar.

'Great! You've beaten us to it. I hope we are not late?' said Nigel.

'No. We've only just arrived ourselves and are recovering from a laughing fit as we mistook a couple who came out of a cab a few minutes ago, for you,' said Burnty.

'You do both look radiant,' complimented Astrid.

'Thank you,' said Emily.

Astrid and Nigel were smartly dressed too. Astrid was wearing a white collarless shirt with a pink flowery design on it over a pair of black trousers. She wore heavy make-up and carried a black handbag which she handed over at the cloakroom for safe-keeping. Nigel was wearing a grey, two-piece suit with a dark blue long-sleeved shirt. They sat down together while they had their drinks. Emily, Burnty and Astrid were drinking white wine, while Nigel had ordered orange juice again.

'How's Chloe?' inquired Burnty.

'She's fine, thank you. She's at home with her grandparents,' responded Astrid.

'Do your parents live in Leicester too?' asked Burnty.

'No, I mean Nigel's parents who we came to visit,' said Astrid.

'My parents live in Biarritz, in the South of France. They moved there about two years ago.'

'Really? I didn't realize that, I assumed that your parents still lived in the UK,' said Emily as she sipped her wine.

'My dad's younger sister got married to a Frenchman who lived in Biarritz. My parents had always got on very well with them, so when they retired, they decided to move to the South of France so that they could all be close together,' said Astrid.

As Emily got up to readjust her seat, a young woman approached her and said, 'Excuse me. Were you the doctor who treated my son at the Royal Infirmary about six months ago?'

Emily looked surprised and not knowing what to expect said, 'Well, maybe. I do work at the Royal Infirmary, but I'm sorry, I don't recognize you. We see so many patients and their relatives every day it is difficult to remember everyone.'

'I just wanted to say thank you. You were very kind that day,' said the young woman.

'Thank you for your kind words,' said Emily looking discomfited. She resumed her seat when the woman had walked away.

Emily thanked her stars that she always tried to be nice to her patients, even when under pressure. She imagined how she would have felt if the encounter had been a negative one.

'Does that kind of thing happen often?' asked Nigel.

'It's not very common, but some grateful patients like to go out of their way to show appreciation,' said Burnty.

'Astrid, what was it like at the World Bank, in terms of working in a multinational environment?' asked Emily, trying to divert attention from herself.

'I enjoyed it. I worked with colleagues from all over the world and it was quite exciting. I remember a lady from Lima in Peru who worked in the same office as I did in Copenhagen. She never knew that I had any link with South America until one day when we all went out to Tivoli and I mentioned that my mum came from Honduras. You could see how excited she was when she found out. After that outing we became very close friends. Her husband, who was Danish, worked at the Ministry of Health in Copenhagen,' said Astrid.

They continued chatting as people came in and out of the bar. 'I'm hearing some music now, it's almost ten o'clock, which is when the dance floor usually opens,' said Nigel.

'Are you a good dancer,' asked Emily, as she got up to go to the toilet.

'Well, I try,' said Nigel smiling.

As Emily walked towards the toilets, she saw a notice that read:

TO REACH THE TOILETS, PLEASE
USE THE STAIRCASE
MANAGEMENT

As she read the signs, she saw a man pass by, wearing a white long-sleeved shirt. Emily followed the signs and entered one of the empty cubicles. Her body went cold as the man had reminded her of Richard with whom she had had a one-night stand while Burnty was in Nigeria. She suddenly became overwhelmed and consumed by pangs of guilt. She started by blaming her parents for making her so vulnerable to any little show of affection, then began to rationalize that after all she did not know what Burnty had been up to while he was in Nigeria. This thought only made her feel worse because she knew quite well that Burnty was faithful to her.

The TV in the corner of the bar was showing a football match between Nigeria and Ghana. 'I like watching football matches involving Nigeria. The country seems to produce a lot of talented players,' said Nigel, as they watched one of the Nigerian players score a goal. 'I remember England and Nigeria met during the 2002 World Cup. It was a tense moment as I was not able to openly support England in my usual uproarious manner out of respect for a Nigerian guest who had come to visit us, and my guest felt the same way too. So we both ended up being neutral, and as if our mood had an impact on the players, the match ended in a draw.'

'I agree with you Nigel, Nigerians are very passionate about football, just like the English. I used to play football for my school team until I was injured,' said Burnty.

Emily was now back from the toilet and she re-joined them.

'What have you been talking about while I've been gone?' enquired Emily heartily, trying to defuse her feelings of internal tension.

'The men have been talking about football. A very macho thing, isn't it?' said Astrid jocularly and they all burst out laughing.

They all went upstairs to join the dancing, as the music was now blaring out loudly.

The Bluefast Nightclub was only for members and their guests, and because of the strict rules for joining, outbreaks of violence during disco sessions were quite rare, which made it attractive to many people. Its location on the London Road, which was not too far from the train station was an added advantage because people from outside Leicester could get there easily.

The manager of the club, Dwight Duncan, a Yorkshireman, was always around and he was good at dealing with any complaints from members. He always saw to it that his staff maintained a high level of decorum and his office was usually inundated with commendation letters from impressed members and their guests. Sometimes he went upstairs to dance and mingle with the clientele.

'Is Dwight around today?' Burnty asked Damian, one of the DJs.

'No. His father-in-law had emergency surgery yesterday at the Royal Infirmary, so he's off today,' said Damian. 'But he'll be back by Monday.'

'We are so sorry!' said Nigel.

'Don don do dodo don do! Don don do dodo don . . .' rang Burnty's cell phone. He dashed downstairs to answer it.

'Hello, *Burnty*,' came the voice from the other end.

It was Burnty's younger brother, Robert, who was calling from Baltimore where he was doing his residency training in internal medicine at the Johns Hopkins Hospital.

'Hey! How are you? It's almost midnight here and I am at a nightclub with Emily and some friends. We were about to get onto the dance floor when you rang,' said Burnty.

'Do you still have time to socialize? It's almost impossible for me because we are so busy here. In fact, my girlfriend has been complaining bitterly about our lack of time for each other. I just hope she doesn't leave me,' said Robert while he chuckled to himself.

'I'm sure that you'll cope. The new EU directive imposed a maximum number of hours per week, above which employees are legally not allowed to work – that's why we have time to socialize now. I'm sure that things will improve when you become an Attending Physician,' said Burnty.

'Are you still in touch with Azuchukwu, your Ibo friend from Enugu?'

'Oh, you mean Azu? He runs a private dental practice in Port Harcourt and is now a multi-millionaire.'

'That's amazing. How did he do it? Did he set up soon after finishing his National Youth Service Corp? He is very lucky.'

'Azu did residency training in orthodontics at the University of Benin Teaching Hospital after he was turned down by the University College Hospital in Ibadan. Then after he completed his training he joined with one of his colleagues, who specialized in maxillofacial surgery, and they set up the private practice in Port Harcourt. From what I have heard, they were able to do so well within a short space of time because they offered specialist services to clients like Shell and Mobil Oil and other multi-national companies in Port Harcourt,' said Burnty. 'He is married now with three kids. His wife is Ebira, from Okene, in Kogi State. She is also a dentist. They met while she was an undergraduate at the University of Benin, while he was a resident dentist. That's life. Each of us has his own destiny. I'm still battling to get the post of a specialist registrar. But I'm quite happy and full of optimism, and I'm confident that good things will eventually come my way.'

'At least you are in a relationship and I do hope that it works out well for both of you. I'm certain that your time will come. Thank you for your efforts during mummy's illness. It was quite a difficult time for me and I couldn't travel even though I wanted to. God will reward your efforts and those of our other siblings. I'll let you go now so that you can join Emily and your friends.'

'OK. Thank you for phoning again. I'll speak to you soon. Goodnight from here. I know that you guys are several hours behind us,' said Burnty.

'Goodnight,' said Robert and he hung up.

Burnty put his phone back in his pocket and dashed towards the staircase to join the others on the dancefloor. As he climbed the staircase, he tripped on a banana skin which had been left on the steps and fell backwards, landing headlong on the floor below. The chairs in the area were scattered and there was instant commotion as everybody rushed to help him.

Burnty was lying on the floor barely able to speak coherently, though he was able to move alright. He was breathing heavily and his head was swollen. An ambulance was called while first aid was being administered by the club's paramedic.

Meanwhile, Astrid and Nigel were busy dancing upstairs and still expecting Burnty and Emily to join them. They had no idea that anything was amiss.

It was only moments later when a woman came up to the dancefloor to tell her friend what had happened, that it suddenly dawned on them that something was wrong.

Astrid and Nigel had heard some noise downstairs but they never suspected anything. They had been dancing close to the doorway and the music was quite loud. Emily had gone downstairs to get something from her bag, which was in the cloakroom, a few minutes after Burnty tripped and fell. She had seen people huddled together, but she did not know why. She had thought that Burnty was still speaking to his brother, Robert. She knew that Burnty liked to talk on the phone for ages especially to his relatives and close friends. It was when she was about to go up again that she decided to find out what was going on, and saw Burnty lying there. She nearly fainted.

'God, what am I seeing? No, no it can't be . . .' shouted Emily and she started to cry. She held on to Burnty's hands and called out his name.

Burnty managed to respond but he was quite dazed.

Moments later, the ambulance arrived and he was taken to the A&E department at the Royal Infirmary, with Emily by his side. It was around 2.30 a.m. by the time they arrived in the hospital. Burnty was promptly seen by the senior house officer, who had already bleeped the on-call surgical and trauma teams. Luckily, the consultant neurosurgeon, Mr Setu Drumstain, was still in the hospital. He had just left the operating theatre and was writing up his notes. Also, the consultant radiologist, Dr Eugene Hansen, had just been called in to do a CT scan on another patient. Burnty was diagnosed as having a head injury and he was sent to the radiology department for an urgent CT scan of the brain, which revealed a collection of blood.

After he was assessed by Mr Drumstain, an arrangement was made for an urgent operation. After all the necessary preparations had been made, Burnty was moved to the operating theatre where the blood collection was drained and he was then transferred to intensive care. After the operation, he was quite conscious. As he was being transferred to intensive care, with Emily walking by his side looking enormously distressed and shattered, Nigel and Astrid appeared. They both looked quite flustered and completely lost for words. They waited outside, since they were not allowed into the intensive care unit, and Emily waved at them and signalled that she would join them later.

'How about Astrid and Nigel?' asked Burnty in a very sluggish and low-toned voice.

'They are waiting in the corridor, as they are not allowed in here,' said Emily.

Emily held Burnty's hand and kissed it, then stroked his cheeks, making sure he was settled comfortably before she went outside to see Astrid and Nigel who both looked very worried. They only found out what had happened after the ambulance had left for the hospital and they immediately followed in a taxi. But by the time they arrived, Burnty had been transferred to the operating theatre, so they had waited around until the operation was over.

'What actually happened?' asked Nigel, who looked shaken and distraught.

'Burnty hasn't been able to tell me yet. All I could gather was that he fell and landed headlong in the smoking area on the ground floor. He was not able to remember everything that happened when he was seen by the doctors. I wanted to make sure he was okay before asking him about the details,' said Emily, who was trying very hard to brighten up and look cheerful.

'What a horrible end to a very promising evening. Thank God he is in a stable condition,' said Astrid.

Astrid was holding on tightly to Nigel's hand for support as her legs began to wobble.

She looked terribly shaken. Astrid had always had a fear of and loathing for hospitals ever since her only brother had died in infancy in a French hospital while they were on holiday with her parents in the South of France many decades ago. He had been buried there and she knew that was another reason why her parents had decided to move to Biarritz, apart from wanting to be close to her aunt and uncle.

'That's what matters. We'll look forward to his speedy recovery. Are we allowed to see him briefly before we go?' asked Nigel.

'Let me ask permission from the nurses and the doctors on duty,' said Emily.

She then dashed back into the intensive care unit and came out about five minutes later to tell Nigel and Astrid that they could go in to see Burnty.

'Burnty, I'm completely lost for words. I simply do not know what to say, other than that we are very happy that you are in a stable condition. Our thoughts are with you and we trust that you will get better soon,' said Nigel as he struggled to hold back tears.

'I'm . . . so sorry . . .' said Astrid. She burst into tears and had to be comforted by Nigel and Emily.

'Thank you,' said Burnty, in a weak voice.

Emily then saw Nigel and Astrid to the car park where a black cab was waiting to take them home, before coming back to join Burnty. Since they were both members of staff of the hospital,

Emily was given an on-call room in which to rest and have some sleep. It was now Sunday morning and she was due to start work when her annual leave ended on the Monday.

When Burnty fell asleep, Emily walked to the on-call room to rest. It was only after she got there that she let herself fall apart, kicking off her shoes, collapsing on the bed and bursting into tears. She wept uncontrollably, as she began to question whether it was the jinx of her brief affair with Richard that was tearing her relationship apart. She felt as if the weight of the whole universe was now on her shoulders.

She began to remember all the painful experiences of her life as far back as her childhood. It was like catharsis for her. She thought of several episodes of domestic violence which she had witnessed at home when she was growing up and how traumatic they were at the time. She had always been the sensitive type which made her susceptible to bullying at school by her school-mates. As she ruminated over all these incidents, she felt an urge to phone her sisters and mum to tell them what had happened to Burnty. But, on checking her watch, she saw that the time was 5.45 a.m., so she decided to go to sleep instead, and call them later in the day.

Emily woke up after a few hours' sleep and she showered and dressed before visiting Burnty. She found him looking much brighter and quite alert. He had just spoken to the doctors who were looking after him and he was able to give them some details of the accident. However, he could only remember speaking to his brother on the phone, tripping on the staircase and falling, then finding himself in hospital.

He contemplated what could have happened to him had he not received prompt medical attention. He was reluctant to inform his family in Nigeria about his hospitalization because he did not want to upset them. But he allowed Emily to phone his cousin, Dominic, who was living in London.

When the doctors and the nurses arrived to do their rounds, Emily left for home.

But on reaching their house, she started feeling lonely and wished she had someone with her. She began to think of the wonderful times she had had with Burnty and found herself reminiscing about their love-making sessions. She wondered how appropriate it was to be thinking of sex at such a time but, she also accepted that sex was part of the fulfilment of their relationship or any relationship between two lovers. Afterall, she thought, sex was one of the physiological needs of human beings like food, clothing and shelter, but it was often left unmentioned.

But, a worrying thought kept on creeping into her mind: she wanted to see Richard again, even though she knew it was wrong, especially now that Burnty was in hospital. Her need to be with someone whenever she was going through stressful moments always overpowered her sense of propriety. She rang her sisters first. She got through to Helen in Truro and she was also able to speak to her husband. But Lala, who was in Hollywood, had gone out with her husband. She dialled her mother's number but it went straight to the answering machine. As she was desperate to speak to her, she dialled her cell phone number and she got through. Her mother was on holiday with her husband in Athens and they had planned to stay for a second week. But, as soon as she told her mother about what had happened to Burnty, they both agreed that they should cut short their holiday so that Emily's mother could fly to Britain to be with her, knowing how stressful it would be for Emily to stay at home alone.

Her mother, Pamela, understood that her need for emotional

support had always been different from that of her other siblings, especially during stressful moments. Emily had protested when her mother said they would cut short their holiday, and she had told her not to, but, inwardly, she was filled with joy when her mother insisted on coming to join her.

She was reluctant to tell her father what had happened because in the past he had been opposed to her dating Burnty. Her father, Nathaniel, had wanted her to marry his friend's son, Clement, who was an Australian living in London. He had introduced them many years ago but no spark had developed between them, so the relationship never took off at all. Since then it seemed to her that her father was secretly pleased when her relationships floundered as it made her look incapable of maintaining a relationship without his advice. He had done the same to her sisters and while it had worked out for Helen, it didn't for Lala. And for this reason, he and Lala were not on speaking terms with each other. He adored Helen because his idea of controlling her relationship had succeeded.

As Emily could not take her mind off Richard she decided to do something about it. She went in search of the brochure he had given her when they met many months before, which contained a list of his Fitness Centres in the UK. She was able to locate the one in Leicester, which was in Walnut Street, and she decided to become a member hoping to use it as a ploy to rekindle her affair with him.

'Shrrh! Shrrh! . . .' rang the phone and Emily rushed to pick up the handset.

'Hello,' said Emily, wondering who it was.

'Emily, I'm so sorry that I missed your phone call. Allen and I have just come in and I was so worried when I heard your message that I decided to ring you right away. Are you alright?' It was Lala, Emily's youngest sister.

'Thank you, Lala. It's very kind of you to ring back so quickly. I'm doing fine now, but yesterday night was horrible. I cried all night and I was desperate to speak to all of you, but it was about 5.45 in the morning here so I decided to wait,' said Emily.

'How did it happen? And how is Burnty doing now?'

'After having some drinks in the bar of a nightclub, we were heading upstairs to the dancefloor, when Burnty had to go back down to take a phone call. We didn't know what was happening downstairs, because the music was very loud but it seems that Burnty fell on the stairs. I only went back down by chance and I accidentally encountered the whole scenario,' said Emily. 'It was absolutely horrifying. But, his condition is now stable.'

'Oh, poor guy! He's such a nice chap. Allen often talks about him since we visited you in Leicester, and they had only met once.'

'I actually came back from the hospital less than three hours ago and I'm due to go back again at 4 o'clock. I've spoken to mummy and Helen and they were both shocked about the news. Mummy has promised to come and see me within the next few days, to spend some time with me. I was secretly delighted, even though I told her not to cut short her holiday.

'Was she on holiday? I last spoke to mummy about four weeks ago.'

'Yes. They were in Athens. They had been there for about a week and were planning to stay for two.'

'Have you told daddy?'

'No! No!! Why should I, when I know that he'll be unsympathetic. After things didn't work out with Clement he hasn't taken kindly to any of my relationships, you know what he's like.'

'Don't mind him. He doesn't seem to realize that we are all different. It was good that it worked out for Helen, but it didn't for me. Can you remember the guy he introduced me to?' Lala burst out laughing.

'Yes, I do,' Emily began to laugh too.

'He's got a strong aversion to foreigners and I don't know why, after all, he lives in Australia. Maybe he thinks it is not a foreign country because Australia has such strong links with the UK.'

'I guess it must be something to do with his childhood. You know our grandfather was Portuguese and that he emigrated to Britain and married our English grandmother. He spoke no English when he arrived in Britain and had to learn it from scratch. For the rest of his life, he spoke English with a thick Portuguese accent and father was always picked on and bullied by his schoolmates who taunted him about his father's accent.'

'Do you think that could really have affected him?' asked Lala.

'I think so. You know that behind that façade of aloofness and stoicism, dad is quite a sensitive person. Those taunts and the derogatory comments which he had to endure did affect him, because he said he vowed to himself that he would not marry a foreigner when he grew up.'

'But who did he marry after he left mummy? A possessive bitch, who doesn't want him to be reconciled with his first family out of pathological jealousy! I'm quite prepared to speak to him whenever he's ready. Vindictivenes and malice are maladies that belong to those who are frustrated and unhappy with their lives. I'm a successful actress with a happy family of my own, caring sisters and a loving mother. He is the one who is trapped in a relationship that does not give him any fulfilment. I really pity him.' Despite her words, Lala sounded despondent.

'He did ask after you when he last spoke to Helen. He is desperate to speak to you but his ego is preventing him from doing so, because of his previous posturings when he failed to impose Kenneth on you.'

'Do you know what I later discovered about his "Mr Right" by sheer chance after I was married to my own Mr Right, my lovely Allen?'

'No, I don't.'

'Kenneth was a member of the British National Party which seemed to be completely xenophobic, even though Britain is a multi-racial and multi-religious country!'

'You should thank your stars that you didn't end up with him. What a surprise, when he was so well educated too.'

'I've discovered that being prejudiced has nothing to do with how well educated you are,' said Lala. 'For instance, here in the USA, I once met a highly successful actress who told me that she used to be a member of the Ku Klux Klan, until her uncle, who was married to an African-American woman, got her to leave. It was like listening to a piece of fiction when she told me, because she was well known and liked for being non-prejudiced. It just goes to show that people can change their negative attitudes when they get the right sort of help.'

Emily could hear some strange background noises on the line.

'I'm hearing some noise. What is it?'

'Allen's dragging a chair around and I'm trying to light a cigarette.'

'I thought that you had stopped smoking,' Emily sounded surprised.

'You are quite right, I did stop. I only started again last week when we began filming on set. I'm going to stop after this movie.' Lala burst out laughing.

'I'm sure you'll be alright after this one, I know that your job can be very stressful. Let me speak to Allen.'

'Hold on . . .' said Lala, as she beckoned for Allen to take the phone.

'Hi Emily, I'm sorry about what happened to Burnty. He's such a nice guy.'

'Thank you, Allen. He's now in a stable condition and I'll be going to see him in the hospital when I finish speaking to you,' said Emily.

'I'm sure everything will be well, and I wish him a speedy recovery,' said Allen.

'Hold on for Lala.' Allen handed the telephone back to his wife.

'You said that you'll soon be going to the hospital to see Burnty, so please tell him that our thoughts are with him. I think I should let you go now. The kids are sleeping or I'd get them to have a word – they've been aching to speak to you.'

'Send them my love when they wake up.'

'I'll do that. Bye bye,' said Lala and she hung up.

After speaking to Lala and Allen, Emily put on something nice for her visit to Burnty in the hospital. But she was also planning to find the Fitness Centre on Walnut Street before visiting the hospital, when the phone rang again. 'Hello, may I speak to Miss Emily Braithwaite please,' came the voice from the other end of the phone.

'It's *Dr* Emily Braithwaite speaking,' corrected Emily, sounding offended. 'How can I help?'

'I'm one of the nurses from the Intensive Care Unit at the Royal Infirmary. Mr Christopher would like to speak to you.'

'Do you mean Burnty Christopher?' asked Emily. She almost corrected the woman again for using the title of Mr instead of Dr, before she remembered that after passing all the membership examinations of the Royal College of Surgeons, Burnty had reverted to the title Mr.

'Yes,' said the nurse, who sounded clinical.

Burnty was now on the line, and he said, 'Darling, how are you? I just wanted to remind you that I'll need my purple dressing gown, if you could bring it along when you come.'

'No problem. How are you feeling? Your voice sounds much stronger now,' said Emily. 'I feel much better. Thank you.' They chatted for a few minutes before Emily hung up. Having been interrupted by Burnty's phone call, Emily changed her plan. Instead of registering with the Fitness Centre on her own, she decided that it would be better to get Burnty to join with her, even though they were already both members of another health club on Vaughan Way.

Emily checked her watch and found that she still had time for a manicure and pedicure with Clara, her beauty therapist whose shop was not too far away. When she pulled out the drawer in the study and saw Clara's business card, she suddenly remembered that Clara was on holiday for three weeks. Emily had been going to her for over two years and she wasn't keen to go to someone new. Not knowing what to do she went into the study to arrange the books she would need for the following day in order to prepare for a lecture she was giving the next week. She looked forward to going back to work, until the thought of a nurse in the A & E department who habitually antagonized her crept into her mind, and her enthusiasm momentarily turned sour.

The nurse was a white woman from Walsall who was married to an Afro-Caribbean lawyer, and they had four mixed-race children. Apparently, she was the only white woman in the A & E department with mixed-race children and she was enormously proud of this as she felt that it made her somehow unique. She had always gotten on well with Emily, until, she discovered that Emily was going out with Burnty, and then she became hostile towards her.

Emily had always taken this in her stride, even though she knew that it was due to jealousy, which she found difficult to comprehend. She had always maintained her sense of calm whenever the nurse was on duty and she never wavered in her duty to her patients. She promised herself though, that enough was enough, especially now when she was going through a stressful situation due to Burnty's hospitalization.

Emily came out of the study and drove to the hospital to see Burnty. When she arrived at the hospital she ran into one of her colleagues, Dr Miranda Barrat, who worked in the gynaecology department.

'Hi Emily. It's nice to see you. How was your leave? I'm sorry about what happened to Burnty, I only heard about it this morning. I've been to see him on the ward and we had a good chat,' said Dr Barrat.

'Thank you, Miranda. It's nice to see you too. My leave was going well until Burnty had his accident. Anyhow, I'll be back at work tomorrow.'

'Oh, that's nice. By the way, you'll be pleased to hear that the nasty nurse in A & E has been transferred to the psychiatry ward.'

'Really? It serves her right. She was an absolute nightmare!' said Emily, she was thrilled with the news. 'When you come to work you want to have as stress-free a day as possible and not have to deal with someone like her.'

'Everyone knew that the reason she used to pick on you was because she was jealous of your relationship with Burnty.'

'But I find that completely baffling.'

'It's quite strange but it's all part of the dark manifestation of human behaviour.'

'I can see that you are on your way home. Will you be on duty tomorrow?'

'Yes. I'll be on night duty.'

'Okay, goodbye.'

'Goodbye,' said Dr Barrat and she walked away.

On reaching intensive care, Emily found Burnty sitting up in bed eating a meal of rice and beef stew and vegetable salad.

He was very pleased to see her.

'You look much better. How long do they want to keep you here before they move you to the main ward?' asked Emily, as she unzipped a bag and got out some of the items she had brought for him.

'They are waiting for the results of my repeat blood urea and electrolytes test. They were not happy with the level of potassium in the last results, so they wanted to be sure that everything was in order before they transferred me to the neurosurgical ward. If the U&E results are fine then they'll probably transfer me to the main ward by tomorrow morning, and if my condition continues to improve, it won't be long before I'm sent home,' Burnty said. He sipped some water from a glass on his bedside table. 'That reminds me, you'll be back at work tomorrow. I'm sure that you're looking forward to it.'

'Of course – if only you were not in hospital. Do you know something? That silly nurse in the A & E department has been transferred to the psychiatry ward.'

'Oh! Do you mean that virago that tried to make your life a misery? God have mercy! You remember that I always encouraged you to try to ignore her idiotic and irritating antics, because she had no right to pick on you the way she did. I expect she'll find someone else to pick on when she gets there.'

Burnty wiped his mouth and kissed Emily, who was now sitting by his bedside.

'She was never an issue in my work, even though she tried to make herself one,' said Emily. 'How about your boss, does he know you're in here?'

'He's been informed by Edith, the specialist registrar, though I intend to speak to him myself as I was due back at work, tomorrow like you.'

'Who is Edith . . . ? Was she the woman whose husband worked in orthopaedic surgery?'

'Yes, she was the one.'

'I thought she was on maternity leave.'

'You're right, I think she just came back. I also learnt that her son has been diagnosed with a congenital heart disease, which means that the poor boy will be needing surgery in the near future.'

'Which disease could it possibly be?'

'I don't know. I think you paediatricians will know.'

'If it's a ventricular septal defect he should be fine, there are excellent cardiothoracic surgeons and paediatric cardiologists in the NHS who'll look after him when the time comes . . .' said Emily, before they were interrupted by one of the nurses.

'Mr Christopher, you look quite cheerful. I'm sure you'll soon be on your way to the main ward,' said Hilda, one of the Intensive Care Unit nurses.

'Are the results of my U&E back?' enquired Burnty.

'Yes, and the level of potassium was normal. The doctors left instructions that you should be transferred to the main ward tomorrow if the potassium level came back as normal,' said Hilda, and she went away to attend to another patient.

'That's great news' said Emily. 'I spoke to Lala and Allen today, and they both said that I should send their love to you.'

'How nice of them. Thank you.' Burnty sounded pleased.

'And my mum promised to come and visit me when I told her what happened. She was on holiday with her husband in Athens.'

'That's very kind of her, but how does her husband feel about it?'

'He's quite happy for her to come. She'll probably only stay for a few days, especially now that your condition is improving so quickly.'

'Have you eaten? I know that you don't eat much.'

'Yes, I've had something to eat.'

Burnty started to read some of the poems of Wole Soyinka that Emily had brought him, while she flipped through a copy of *Hello!* magazine. After a while she leant forward and joined Burnty in reading through the poems. They both loved reading poetry; Emily's favourites were William Wordsworth, Ezra Pound and W.B. Yeats.

'Do you enjoy Soyinka's poems?' asked Burnty. 'I know that your favourites are Pound and Wordsworth.'

'His poems are good, but difficult.'

'That's true. In fact some literary critics have described Soyinka as an obscurantist because of his style of writing, but his poems are brilliant.'

'That reminds me, I need to return those poetry books we borrowed from the library. They are long overdue.'

'I thought you had returned them a long time ago,' Burnty looked surprised.

'Actually, I should have, but I kept one of them which was an anthology of Ezra Pound's poems. I enjoyed reading them so much that I was almost reduced to tears. It reminded me of when my dad used to read them to us when he and my mum were still together. I couldn't really understand them then. I remember one occasion when Lala played a prank on my dad. Being the youngest of the three of us, she couldn't begin to fathom what the poems were about, so one day when she knew that it was time for daddy to start his readings, she hid the book. My dad went to the book shelf and he couldn't find it. I never knew that he used to enjoy those sessions himself until he got angry, and then he decided to give us another book to read which was called *Power is Knowledge*. He said, "girls that's your dinner for tonight; enjoy it" and left the room. We all burst out laughing. I remember Helen asked for some cutlery to devour the book. It was absolutely hilarious.'

'Your dad sounds like a fun person.'

'Oh yes, he is. But somehow, he did not get along with my mum. I don't know whether it was because they both had strong and uncompromising personalities. I believe that, for any relationship to work, there has to be some compromise between the parties involved. My parents didn't seem to be able to do that for reasons which I did not understand,' Emily was now looking gloomy.

Burnty tried to change the subject when he saw the change in Emily's mood. He knew how emotional Emily got whenever she discussed her parents' marriage. On most occasions, she usually ended up bursting into tears. She always said that she had been deeply affected by the break-up of her parents' marriage. This was worsened by the fact that she was the only one in her class at school whose parents were divorced, until Astrid arrived. She acknowledged that Helen and Lala had coped very well and never seemed to have been as affected by it as she was.

'We are happy together now and I think you should be able to draw some strength from that,' said Burnty. 'I think all marriages have their problems, which I believe is intrinsic in the very fact of two people coming together to live together as one unit. There are bound to be disagreements and differences of opinion, but the ability to rise above these differences and maintain a common ground is what I believe makes any successful marriage work. My parents had differences too, and they still do, but they are usually able to reach a compromise. Sometimes, my dad will yield ground and on other occasions my mum will. Trouble comes into a marriage when both parties refuse to yield ground to each other and sometimes this can happen over the most inconsequential of issues.'

They were then interrupted by Hilda, who said, 'I'm sorry to interrupt you, Mr Christopher. I just wanted to check your medication with you. Your analgesics have been changed to oral and we are still expecting your liver function test results, which should hopefully arrive after you've been transferred to the main ward.'

'That's alright. Thank you,' said Burnty.

The nurse then walked away.

'Why are they doing LFTs?' queried Emily.

'It was because I complained of upper abdominal pains, yesterday. But, they have since stopped.'

Emily stayed with Burnty and they chatted about many things until it was late in the evening. Then Emily left for home to prepare for her return to work the following day.

6

Burnty was transferred to the neurosurgical ward as scheduled after his liver function test results came back as normal. He was delighted to be in the general ward where most of the patients were not as sick as those in intensive care. His neighbour on the ward was a GP who was actually under the care of the plastic surgeons. He had been treated for first degree burns to his lower limbs. He and Burnty hit it off straightaway, but he was discharged two days after Burnty arrived on the ward.

Meanwhile, Burnty's cousin, Dominic, who lived in London had already phoned to inform him that he was on his way to see him in the hospital. Burnty gave him directions to his ward. Dominic had been monitoring Burnty's condition by phone since he could not come immediately after the accident happened. As Burnty read through the newspapers, he went through in his mind what he had left undone. He had already spoken to his boss who was quite sympathetic and he was now officially on sick leave. Emily had returned to work and she had been to see him earlier in the day. He saw an article in *The Times* that really interested him. It was about the difficulties that foreign-trained doctors and dentists faced in the NHS. He also began to review in his mind the interviews that he had scheduled. Luckily, none of them was earlier than four weeks away. He was, however, still keeping the news of his accident from his relatives. Apart from Robert, his younger brother in the USA, and Dominic, all his other relatives were unaware of the accident. He wanted to be discharged first before telling them about it.

'Good afternoon, Mr Christopher. My name is Sintawara; I am one of the nurses who will be looking after you on the ward. I just wanted to cross-check a few things with you. By the way this is your wrist band which you need to wear now.'

'Thank you.'

After asking Burnty a few questions the nurse said, 'The doctors will see you later.'

'Thank you,' said Burnty, and he continued reading the news-papers. He flicked through the *Daily Telegraph* where he saw an article about the opening of a new multi-million pound hospital for children in Lokoja, Kogi State in Nigeria; he was very impressed by the project. The article also addressed the issue of the brain drain and its impact on healthcare delivery in Nigeria. When he had finished reading the article, Burnty started watching the television, which was showing a programme about home ownership and property prices in various parts of the UK. He was interrupted by Dr John Finlay, one of the doctors on duty.

'Good afternoon, Mr Christopher, I'm Dr Finlay. I'm one of the senior house officers on the ward under Mr Drumstain, the consultant-in-charge. I understand that you were transferred to the ward today. I've gone through all the results of your tests and we'll be keeping you under close observation. If things continue as they are, you may be on your way home very soon. As of today, all your results are normal,' said Dr Finlay. 'I'm also aware that you are a research fellow in maxillofacial surgery in this hospital.'

'That's correct, and are you one of the new senior house officers?'

'Yes. I used to work in Birmingham Heartlands Hospital. I'm on a surgical rotation and my last job there was in urology.'

'What speciality do you hope to go into after your membership examinations?'

'I don't know yet. This is my second posting since I finished internship last year. I'm thinking of either colo-rectal or upper gastrointestinal surgery. I'll see how things go by the time I finish the three-year rotation.'

'You are very lucky. You don't have to apply for jobs every six months, as doctors who can't get into a rotation have to do.'

'That's quite true. I remember one of my colleagues during my last job in urology. He told me that he could not get into a rotation and he was actually doing a trust grade job. He was a foreign-trained doctor. If I may ask, where did you train?'

'I trained in the University of Lagos in Nigeria for my dental degree and in Nottingham University for my medical qualification. How about you?'

'I trained in the University of Birmingham, here in the UK. So that means that you had to be doubly qualified?'

'Yes.'

'Anyway, it's been nice speaking to you, Mr Christopher. I'll have to go and see my other patients now.'

'I wish you the best. See you tomorrow.'

'Thank you,' said Dr Finlay, and he walked away.

After Dr Finlay left him Burnty got out of bed, put on his

slippers and went to the toilet. As he was coming back, he saw Dominic, who was walking towards the nurses' station. He called out excitedly, 'Dominic, I'm here.'

'Burnty, how are you? I'm so happy to see you. You look well. It's been terribly busy for me in the office and my boss would not let me out of his sight for one second or I'd have been here sooner. I've been worried ever since you told me, even though you reassured me that all was well,' said Dominic.

'I'm getting better day by day.'

Burnty led him to his bed.

'After I spoke to you yesterday, I talked to Emily. She told me that you were being transferred to this ward today. So I knew where to find you.'

Dominic was now seated on a chair by Burnty's bedside.

'Your head is still bandaged. I hope you are not in too much pain? I'm a layman when it comes to medical issues,' said Dominic, looking concerned.

'It's much better now. The pain has subsided and all my blood tests and radiological reports have come out as normal. How's your wife, Isabel?'

'She's doing fine. She's gone to see her parents in Ulm.'

'Ulm? I thought her parents lived in Stuttgart,' said Burnty, looking surprised.

'Yes, you're right. They actually originate from Ulm and that's where Isabel was born. But she grew up in Stuttgart, where her parents ran an art gallery before they retired and went back to Ulm.'

'Were her parents artists too?'

'Yes. Her father was a famous painter in Germany and her mother was a talented sculptor. She comes from a family of artists – one of her brothers and both of her sisters are artists. Her other brother trained as a doctor and is a gynaecologist in Munich.'

'This Ulm also rings a bell for another reason but I cannot quite remember why.' Burnty's head was raised as if he was trying to recollect something.

'That'll be because Albert Einstein, the renowned physicist, was born in Ulm. Isabel was always proud of the fact that they shared a common birthplace.'

'Yes you are right, it's Albert Einstein. I found that out when I was researching the biographies of Nobel Prize winners in physics when I was preparing for an essay competition in my first year at the University of Lagos.'

Burnty heaved a sigh of relief and looked pleased that Dominic had helped him to remember.

'So, when are they planning to discharge you?'

'One of the junior doctors came to see me not long before you arrived. He told me that all my results were normal and that if things remained satisfactory I might be going home soon. I won't get my hopes up too much until the consultant's ward round tomorrow.'

'Who's the consultant?'

'It's a Mr Drumstain.'

'Where's he from?'

'I really don't know. I guess he's British but I'm not too sure. So far he's been very nice and courteous.'

'I'm concerned about this MRSA which they sensationalize in the newspapers.'

'Don't worry. It's usually over-hyped and blown out of all proportion by the media,' Burnty laughed. 'What time is your train back to London?'

'The last one leaves at 8.30 p.m.,' said Dominic as he browsed through the books arranged on Burnty's bedside table.

'That's fine.'

'Have you read Rudyard Kipling's poem *If*?' asked Dominic, when he spotted the poem in an anthology on Burnty's table.

'Yes, I have. It's quite interesting, and I have also read a different version of it which was written by another British poet.'

'Was it the man who was said to have turned down a KBE some years ago?'

'Yes, he was the one. What do you make of that, as someone whose country was colonized by the British?'

'Well, people are entitled to their own opinions, which I think should be respected. Personally, I am quite neutral. I believe that changes to such titles that date back centuries can only be gradual. The pros and cons of colonialism and its impact on the people of the countries colonized will continue to be a subject for debate. I know that it can be a quite touchy subject for those from countries that had to fight wars of liberation before they gained their independence, unlike Nigeria and Ghana, which got theirs by negotiation. On the whole, I think people should have the right to accept or decline any award that is bestowed on them, since that's part of the exercise of their human rights,' said Dominic.

'There are many ways to look at it. When you view colonialism in the context of world history, it is similar to all the wars that have been motivated by the desire to conquer and dominate other people. In that sense it is just like the Norman Conquest of 1066, which is a key date in British history. I believe that we should move on and not remain fixated on the historical ills of the past. I am aware that the repercussions of colonialism are still there to see, but so are those of other events like the First and Second World Wars, which devastated Europe. At the end of the day, as you rightly pointed out, the right of individuals to refuse or accept honours should be respected,' said Burnty.

'I think I agree with you.'

'You seem to be quite conversant with human rights issues. I know that you've always been interested in issues concerning fair play. Shouldn't you study law?'

'I might look into that . . .' joked Dominic, before he was interrupted by the ringing of his cell phone.

After pressing the answer button he said, 'Hello, this is Dominic.'

'How are you darling? I'm calling from Dusseldorf. You told me that you'll be going to see your cousin, Burnty. How was he?' It was Isabel, Dominic's wife.

'Honey, how marvellous to speak to you. He's doing fine. In fact, I'm here with him on the ward and he's been asking after you. You've gone to Dusseldorf already? I thought you said that you were all meeting in Ulm?'

'That's right. But my sister, Leonora, couldn't join us in Ulm. Her mother-in-law came to visit them and she had to be rushed to hospital with severe abdominal pains. She was diagnosed with an intestinal obstruction and had to be operated on, so my sister stayed behind to look after her. That's why I had to travel to see her before returning to the UK.'

'How's her condition now? I mean your sister's mother-in-law?'

'She is in a stable condition and is making good progress.'

'How are your parents?'

'Mummy and daddy are doing fine. They sent their love to you. Daddy said that I should remind you about that book you both discussed when you last met in London. He refused to tell me which book it was; he simply said that you'd know about it.'

'Oh! It's a book about Hans Holbein. Your dad is quite passionate about Holbein, possibly because he was German.'

'Ah, now I know why he refused to tell me about it. He knew that I'm more inclined to non-German painters and he didn't want me to tease him.' Isabel burst out laughing. 'Please let me speak to Burnty.'

'Hi, Isabel. I would love to be able to speak to you in German, but unfortunately my German is simply atrocious. How are you and your family in Germany?' asked Burnty.

'They are doing fine. I'm happy to hear that your condition has greatly improved, and I'm sure that all will be well with you. I hope Emily is coping well. I hear that she's back at work now. You're sounding good; I hope they won't keep you in for too long.'

'Thank you. I hope so too. So far my test results have been fine. Emily has gone back to work. We were both supposed to go back at the same time but then I had the accident. When are you returning to the UK? I'm sure Dominic is missing you terribly.' Burnty glanced at Dominic and saw him smiling.

'Very soon. I'm on the last leg of my trip. So I'll see you when I come back to London.'

'I wish you a safe journey back to the UK. Let me hand over the phone to Dominic,' said Burnty.

'Honey, I'm dying to see you. I'll phone daddy and mummy when I get back to London,' said Dominic.

'When are you going back?'

'Tonight.'

'Why so soon, didn't Mr Huskett give you a day off to go and see Burnty?'

'No. You know what he's like, especially during busy times like now? He bluntly refused and Burnty understands anyhow, so I have to go back tonight.'

'That's fine. I wish you a safe journey home.'

'Thank you; I wish you the same,' said Dominic finally before the line went dead.

'Dominic, it's almost six o'clock now, I think I should let you get back to London,' said Burnty, as he got out of bed and went to speak to a nurse.

'That's true.'

When Burnty returned, Dominic was ready to leave and Burnty only went with him to the door as the doctors had told him not to venture too far.

'The taxi rank is by the main hospital entrance. Thank you for coming. We'll talk again when you arrive in London.'

'Take care and continue to stay cheerful. I know that you don't need any advice about that. Goodbye.'

They shook hands, then Dominic left to get a taxi to the station.

Burnty came back to the ward and stood by one of the windows looking out. The neurosurgical ward was on the second floor; directly overlooking the hospital car park, where he had always parked his car whenever he was on duty. He never once imagined that he would be a patient on the very ward where he worked. He saw some pigeons flying around and noticed some hospital staff who were rushing home. This made him think of Emily who had gone home to work on her impending lecture. She had about three years left before she became a consultant paediatrician. Burnty also thought about his own career and could only hope for the best. After all, he still had lots of interviews lined up and he almost got one of the jobs he was interviewed for two months earlier, only one of his referees was on holiday and didn't send the reference on time. Burnty was not one to apportion blame, so he just took it in his stride even though he was deprived of a job offer as a result of this. Being an eternal optimist, he believed that he only had to persevere and that his time would eventually come.

He looked at the houses outside the hospital grounds, some of which were detached houses with elegant gardens. He suddenly remembered that one of his consultants lived in one of the houses and he began to think of the mortgage payments on the house he shared with Emily.

After a while, Burnty left the window and went back to lie in bed. He was a fatalist and this philosophy had helped him to cope with the vicissitudes of life. It had made him more accepting of whatever fate threw at him, especially those things beyond his control. He was interrupted in his thoughts by his neighbour.

'Hi, Mr Christopher. My name is Sonny. How are you today?' said the patient whose bed was next to his.

'Hi, I'm Burnty. Please call me Burnty. I'm doing all right. I see you arrived today.'

'Yes, you're right. I'm due to have an elective operation under the general surgeons tomorrow,' said Sonny. 'I hope they will do it so that I can return to work soon. I am a plumber and my company's got a big building construction project going on just now.'

'I hope so too.'

'I can see that you've been here for a while. What do you do for a living?'

'I am a dental surgeon and I work in this hospital.'

Sonny looked alarmed. 'Doctors get sick too then? I always thought that as they know everything about the human body, they shouldn't get sick.'

'Doctors are human beings too. Anybody can become a patient when taken ill, and doctors are not immune to this.' They both started laughing.

His new neighbour was quite talkative and Burnty enjoyed talking to him. Later as he lay in bed, Burnty stared at the ceiling and thought about his brothers and sisters. He found himself thinking about Robert, who was doing his residency training in the USA.

Robert was his younger brother and he had always known what he wanted to do since he was a child. He once told Burnty that the inspiration to study medicine came to him during one of the visits he and his classmates made to an immunisation centre, when he was at primary school. He had always been clever and he did very well in his O Levels before sitting the Joint Matriculation Examination to study medicine at the University of Ibadan. He was an active sportsman and had played football for his hall of residence.

Burnty, on the other hand, had always been fascinated by teeth, and was encouraged to pursue dentistry by one of his father's friends. As thoughts continued to whirl around his mind, he began to gradually drift off to sleep, until he was suddenly roused by the loud voice of another patient's visitor. He opened his eyes briefly and then finally fell asleep.

Burnty woke up the following morning and, after having a shower, he got dressed and sat by his bedside, looking alert and cheerful. He ate a hearty breakfast of poached egg, toast, baked beans and sausage. Since things had remained the same since he was last seen by Dr Finlay, Burnty hoped that he might be discharged soon. He went to the nurses' station to enquire about the newspaper man who delivered the early morning papers, but he was told that the man was off for the day and the colleague who was standing in for him had not been seen. Burnty went instead to the hospital shop downstairs, where he bought a copy of *The Times* and the *Daily Telegraph*. On his way back upstairs, he met Dwight Duncan, the manager of the Blueshaft Nightclub in the lift. Dwight had come to the hospital to deliver some items to his father-in-law.

'Hello, Mr Duncan,' said Burnty.

Looking a bit surprised, Dwight Duncan said, 'Hello. I'm sorry, I can't remember your name. Are you a member of the Blueshaft?' He couldn't remember Burnty's name, since he dealt with so many customers on a daily basis but, he recognized his face and had heard about the accident.

'Yes. I tripped and fell while I was there with my partner and some friends a few days ago.'

'I'm really sorry. I was told about the accident when I came on duty the following day but unfortunately I couldn't put a face to the name. When I saw you, I knew that I had seen your face before, but it didn't click until you called my name. How are you doing now?'

'I'm doing fine . . .'

They suddenly realized that neither of them had pressed any of the buttons for the various floors.

'Which floor are you going to?' enquired Burnty, pressing the button for the second floor.

'The fourth,' said Dwight.

Burnty pressed the button. Before they had a chance to say much more, the door opened and Burnty got out. 'Goodbye,' he said. 'I'm afraid I need to rush back before the doctors begin their rounds.'

'Goodbye,' said Dwight as the lift doors shut.

Burnty walked back to his ward and met Mr Drumstain, the consultant neurosurgeon, and the other members of his team. They were about to begin the ward round and he walked past them towards his bed to get himself ready for them. Burnty was reading through *The Times* when Mr Drumstain arrived with his team.

'Good morning, Mr Christopher. How are you today?' asked Mr Drumstain, smiling.

'I'm doing fine, thank you,' said Burnty.

'I gather that all your blood test results have come out as normal, but we are still awaiting the radiologist's report of your latest CT scan. I've seen the films though and they look all right and I've spoken to the radiologist about them, so I've left instructions that you should be discharged when the report eventually arrives today. Do you have any questions? Or is there anything that you wish to clarify?'

'Thank you. I just wanted to ask about a sick leave certificate, since I won't be able to go back to work immediately.'

'I'm aware of that and, as a matter of fact, I have spoken to your boss about it. Dr Finlay will sort out the paperwork for you after the ward round.'

'Thank you, Mr Drumstain,' said Burnty as the team proceeded to their next patient. After they were gone, Burnty went outside to bleep Emily and tell her the latest development. After speaking to Emily, who was delighted by the news, he came back to the ward and continued reading the papers. He saw an article in *The Times* about an Olympic swimmer and immediately thought about Astrid and Nigel's daughter, Chloe, who had invited them to her swimming competition. He promised himself that if he was discharged, he and Emily would keep their promise. He remembered how touched he had been when Astrid and Nigel visited him for the second time. They had come to see him again on the very day that he was transferred from intensive care. He had been very happy to see them and they had all chatted away like old friends. They had brought Chloe to see him on their way back to London and she had been very inquisitive, asking questions like that of someone far older. It was not difficult to see how intelligent she was and Burnty was glad that her parents had sent her to a special school for gifted children. She seemed to be interested in mathematics and her teachers had assessed her level to be the equivalent of someone studying for O Level maths. If she continued to get the right coaching, her teachers had predicted that by the time she was thirteen, she would comfortably be able to sit an undergraduate mathematics examination.

Apart from maths, she was also interested in pursuing a career in medicine or engineering, but she wasn't too sure which yet. Her parents definitely made it clear that they would not push her to do anything that she was not interested in, but she seemed to be interested in everything. She told Burnty that she loved her parents' home in Fulham and asked if he had any children.

After Burnty finished reading his newspapers, his thoughts shifted to Dominic again. He wondered what he'd be doing now. They had always been close since Dominic came back to Nigeria from Britain, to continue his education in Ilorin. They were always there for each other. He promised himself that he'd phone Dominic when he was finally discharged. Burnty felt that it was always good to have one's close family around especially during stressful times. Dominic's trip to see him had meant a lot to him.

Dr Finlay came to tell him that the CT scan report had arrived while Burnty was in the middle of doing a crossword puzzle.

'Hello, Mr Christopher, I just wanted to tell you that the radiologist's report of your latest CT scan has arrived and it's normal. As Mr Drumstain told you earlier, we'll be discharging you today. I'll sort out the necessary paperwork with the nurse. You should see your GP for the removal of the sutures. Do you have any questions?' asked Dr Finlay.

'Thank you. I've got no questions.' Burnty was excited.

'Fine. Goodbye and all the best,' said Dr Finlay, as he walked away. Burnty phoned Emily to tell her the good news and then began to gather his things. Emily was still on duty and she promised to drive him home after she finished work. He also phoned his cousin Dominic.

'Hello, this is Dominic Christopher,' came Dominic's voice.

'Dominic, it's me,' said Burnty. 'How are you, and how was your journey back to London yesterday?'

'It wasn't too bad, though it was quite eventful. Have you been discharged yet?'

'Yes. That's part of the reason why I phoned you. What do you mean by eventful?' asked Burnty, with a little frown on his face.

'You wouldn't believe what happened. I boarded the wrong train – the one I got on was going to Liverpool.'

'How did you manage that?'

'I guess they must have changed the platform for the London-bound train at the last minute and I didn't realize because the screen was far away from where I was sitting. So when the train arrived, I just jumped onto it and by the time I realized what was happening we had travelled for an hour and a half and the next stop was miles away. I decided to stay on the train until it arrived at Liverpool.'

'I'm so sorry. Where did you spend the night then?'

'The whole thing turned out to be a blessing in disguise. I had never been to Liverpool before. All I knew about the place was that The Beatles came from there and I love their music. So I decided that it would be a good opportunity for me to pay homage to them by spending the night in Liverpool.'

'I hope that you didn't arrive late at work?'

'Not at all, I stayed at an hotel at the John Lennon Airport and managed to catch an early flight. It's funny how things happen that on the surface might be annoying, but in the end turn out to be for the best. My inadvertent trip to Liverpool was one of them.'

'I know that you are a huge fan of The Beatles and what a nice way to pay homage to them. So what does that make you, an inadvertent traveller or a devoted fan?' teased Burnty.

'I think either would suit me fine,' said Dominic as they both laughed. 'I have some good news for you, so hold your breath.'

'That's great, what's the news?'

Dominic shuffled through the file on his desk to fish out the letter informing him that he had been shortlisted for the final round of the UNESCO International Competition for Sculptors, which he had entered about twelve months earlier.

'I've been invited to Rangoon for the final round of the UNESCO International Competition for Sculptors.'

'What competition is that . . . ?' Burnty was surprised, as Dominic hadn't mentioned it before.

'Well, you didn't know about it. I entered this competition about twelve months ago. It was organized by UNESCO to make a statue in honour of one of the former UN Secretary Generals, U Thant, who was from Burma. The first round was held in Calcutta, and I went there where I won the European category. We were told that only ten of the two hundred contestants would make it through to the final round to be held in Rangoon. And when I arrived in my office this morning, I found this letter on my desk. When I opened it, I couldn't believe my luck!' Dominic paused. 'I'll be travelling to Rangoon in a few months and I'll need all the luck I can get to do well at the event. I'm over the moon, but I haven't told Isabel yet, I'm waiting till she's safely back in London before I break the news. I don't want her to be distracted on the journey home.'

'I'm delighted to hear this. Congratulations! I'm really thrilled for you. You deserve every ounce of your success because you've worked so hard. You have my best wishes at all times and I pray that you'll win when you travel to Rangoon,' said Burnty, his voice heavy with emotion.

'Thank you.'

Burnty and Dominic had always enjoyed each other's successes.

'Burnty, I know you won't mind me cutting you short, my boss wants to see me in a couple of minutes and I need to get ready for our meeting. I'll call you later at home. Send my love to Emily and congratulations on your release from hospital.'

'Thank you. I hope your meeting goes well. Bye,' said Burnty.

After his conversation with Dominic, Burnty gathered his belongings and packed them into a bag. When he had finished he went to the nurses' station to chat with the nurses while he waited for Emily. She arrived about an hour later as soon as she had finished work and they both said a final goodbye to all the staff on the ward and left for home.

7

July 2003

Anonsa and Baguda had just arrived home to their four bedroom house on Albert Street in Dundee. They were both sitting in the living room which had a rich burgundy carpet, where Baguda was sitting pulling off his socks. Anonsa had already taken her shoes off and she wandered into the study to pick up her laptop, which she brought back to the living room. She began to surf some internet websites then checked her email and found a new message. It was from an uncle on her father's side of the family with whom she had lost contact for over ten years. After her father died, some of his family had made trouble for her mother over her father's property because he had died intestate. After that, her mother decided to severe her relationship with them, but this uncle had persisted in visiting them and writing them letters of support. He was her father's youngest brother and was now living in Rio de Janeiro with his second wife, who was Brazilian.

Anonsa read through the email and decided to send him a reply later in the day. Baguda was watching TV and, after switching off her laptop, Anonsa joined him. She sat on the sofa with her legs stretched out on his lap.

'I just finished using my laptop, so I decided to lap it up on your lap,' joked Anonsa, and they both laughed at her joke.

They had not made love for sometime because they had both been very busy with work lately, in fact, this was one of the longest times they had spent without making love since they had been together. Baguda, who was now sexually aroused, drew Anonsa closer to him and put his hands on her breasts. Suddenly a spark went through them and they began to caress and fondle each other urgently. They moved into the bedroom where Anonsa took her top off exposing her large, firm breasts. Baguda had stripped to his underwear, thus revealing his massive bulge. At school he had been nicknamed 'the Cobra' because of the size of his penis. Anonsa began to perform fellatio on him while he groaned with pleasure. When his penis became fully erect he slipped it into her and they made love animatedly. Baguda gave a loud grunt as he climaxed. When he eventually came out Anonsa had semen flowing down her thighs. They both lay in bed looking spent and radiating pleasure. After a while they went into the bathroom and showered, wrapping themselves in huge fluffy, white towels.

After dressing, Anonsa went into the kitchen to make two cups of tea which she took into the sitting room, where Baguda joined her. He began to go through the files that he had brought home from work. His office was located on Albany Terrace, where he worked as a solicitor, while Anonsa was a senior house officer in Ninewells Hospital.

'Haven't you finished with your clients' work yet?'

'No, there are so many of them, and I'm taking them one at a time.'

'I hope that you'll be finished by the time I return from the hairdresser, so that we can go to Thomas Cook and book our holiday in Dublin.'

'That would be good, why don't you go now so that I can work on the files and by the time you come back I might be through with them. We could also go to the Forum Shopping Centre to pick up the printer from Dixons if time permits.'

Anonsa went to change her clothes while Baguda busied himself with the files. When she came back to the sitting room, she planted a kiss on his cheek and then left the house. She got in her car and drove off towards the hairdressers which was on Douglas Street. When she arrived at the salon it was very busy. Since she hadn't made an appointment, she had to wait her turn. She used the time to phone Janet, a former colleague at Ninewells Hospital, who was now working as a specialist registrar in anaesthesia at the Royal Victoria Hospital in Belfast.

'Hi Janet, it's Anonsa speaking,' she said when the call went through.

'Hi Anonsa, how marvellous to hear your voice,' replied Janet. 'You won't believe it, but I was just thinking about my time in Dundee when you phoned. That's amazing. How are you doing?'

'I'm doing fine. In fact, I'm at the hairdressers waiting to get my hair done and I decided to give you a call.'

'I'm sorry I haven't called, it's been so busy here. As you know, I was at the Belfast City Hospital for six months and it was astonishingly busy over there. And to make matters worse, the weekend I was changing to the Royal Victoria Hospital, my husband was admitted to the Erne Hospital in Enniskillen for acute pancreatitis.'

'I'm so sorry, I quite understand why you couldn't call. It might be difficult for someone who is not in this profession to comprehend how busy it can get sometimes. I hope he's all right now?' Anonsa sounded sympathetic.

'Yes, thank you. I was able to have him transferred to the Royal Victoria Hospital to be close to me. His condition improved and he was discharged a few weeks ago. He has since gone back to work. I understand from Theresa that you intend to switch to public health for your specialist registrar training.'

'That's true. You know that I've always valued contact with the larger community. I have been interested in public health since I was in the medical school. Are you in the hospital at the moment? I heard a noise that sounded like a bleep.'

'Yes, I am. I'm actually on-call, but so far it's been very light. I wish you good luck in your choice. I wanted to do gastroenterology myself, but after I did a posting in anaesthesia, I just loved it and I changed my mind. I hope to become an intensivist.'

Just then Janet was bleeped.

'I hear you've been bleeped so I'll let you go. I wish you the best too. Take care, enjoy your on-call duty and send my greetings to your husband. Bye.'

'Goodbye,' said Janet.

Anonsa put her cell phone back into her handbag and shortly after she was called for her hair treatment. She also had a manicure and a pedicure before she drove back home to pick Baguda up for their trip to Thomas Cook.

When Anonsa arrived home Baguda was still busy with his files, but he had only one left, so he abandoned it and they went out. They drove into the city centre where they booked their holiday in Dublin. By that time it was too late to pick up their printer so they drove back home again. When they arrived home Baguda switched on the news.

'History was made today when an archaeological dig in the city of York revealed the fossilized remains of an extinct animal which was estimated to be about five hundred thousand years old. Archaeological researchers and historians are continuing with their investigations . . .'

'How do they know the age?' asked Baguda, sounding incredulous.

'They use a technique called radiocarbon dating in estimating the age of fossil remains.'

'I am quite interested in archaeology. I've often pondered about the origins of man. My younger sister used to talk to me about this as she studied archaeology at the University of York. She is currently on an expedition in Acapulco in Mexico. Her friends who were studying at other universities gave her the nickname "the egg yolk" because she went to York.'

'Which of your sisters are you talking about?'

'The second to youngest. You haven't met her yet.'

'I know that one of your sisters won a silver medal in athletics at the Seoul Olympics in 1988.'

'Actually, it was a bronze medal,' Baguda corrected her.

'Talking of the Olympics, what do you think about the 2008 games due to be hosted by China?'

'I think China is making all the necessary preparations for hosting it, but my sister will not be competing at it. I'm particularly looking forward to the proposed London Olympics in 2012, that's if London wins the final nomination. Can you imagine that the last time it was held in London was in 1948?'

'That's a long time ago. I know that the one in 2004 is to be held in Athens, but I can't remember where it was held before that,' said Anonsa, looking unsure.

'I used to be quite good on the Olympics, let me test my memory. It was held in Sydney, Australia, in 2000; in Atlanta, USA, in 1996; in Barcelona, Spain, in 1992; in Seoul, South Korea, in 1988; in Los Angeles, USA, in 1984; in Moscow, Russia, in 1980; in Montreal, Canada, in 1976; in Munich, Germany, in 1972; in Mexico City, Mexico, in 1968; in Tokyo, Japan, in 1964. I can't remember where it was held in 1960,' said Baguda.

Anonsa looked very impressed. 'You are too good. Don't you think that you should be called "Encyclopedia Olympicus"? I love the Olympics myself, because it represents the entire human race. I remember an advertisement about the Olympics which was on CNN some time ago and it ended with the slogan *"Olympics, celebrating humanity . . ."*'

'I didn't get to see much of the last Olympics. I had to work late for almost three weeks in a row during the games. I also couldn't watch the match between England and Nigeria during the last World Cup.'

'Oh yes, that's right. That was when you were working on that troublesome client who kept being rude to the staff in your office. I hope that you did sort out his case?'

'Your memory is fantastic! We're through with his case, but we do get clients like that from time to time. We always look after them professionally though and they usually end up as satisfied customers, sometimes even dishing out words of commendation. It's all about listening to their grievances and not wishing them away no matter how annoying they might initially seem. They often say that "the customer is always right", and by listening and responding to complaints we rarely go wrong. That was how we were able to handle that particular client. We initially thought he was one of the most difficult clients we had ever seen, but we ended up being proved wrong. It's always important to listen and respond to people's grievances if you hope to work well with them.'

'You sound amazingly didactic. I think that you should take up a part-time lecturing job in one of the law schools.'

'I think I should – in addition to my present crippling workload – that way I can dive straight into the roll of honour of people who suffer a nervous breakdown due to overwork . . .'

'That's interesting, which means that we'll be able to have a funpacked holiday. I'm really looking forward to our holiday,' said Baguda. 'I'll have to quickly book the time off when I go to work, before one of my colleagues picks up the dates.'

Baguda was now working on his last file and he began to think about his family. Being from a mixed-race background, with a white British father and a black British-born mother of Nigerian origin, he felt quite comfortable about his identity. Even though he had been called derogatory names at school, he was never negatively affected by people's comments. Baguda was a very secure person, who was confident and self-assured. He had a very happy childhood, with lots of affection from his parents. Both sets of grandparents also doted on him when he was growing up, especially when they came to visit his parents. He had two younger sisters and two white older half brothers from his father's previous marriage. His parents had met on a trip to do charity work in Dhaka, in Bangladesh. They were both in their twenties at the time and had volunteered to help when Dhaka and other cities in Bangladesh were swamped by a devastating flood. It was while they were relaxing in the hotel lobby they met and they started talking to each other. They had been sent to the hotel by the airline which was due to fly them to Dhaka, after it cancelled their flight. They had stayed in the hotel for forty-eight hours, still hoping to fly to Dhaka, when they were finally told that due to bad weather conditions the trip could not go ahead.

Before leaving for home, they exchanged telephone numbers and soon afterwards began seeing each other. Things snowballed from there and they finally got married. Baguda had been inspired in his choice of career by his mother's cousin, who was a High Court judge in Nigeria and who used to visit them when he was young. They used to talk a lot and he remembered asking the man countless questions. His uncle thought he was very intelligent, so when he later decided to study law at the university, his uncle encouraged him. Baguda was on the last page of his file when his cell phone rang.

'Hi Baggy, how are you?' It was the voice of his younger sister, Dawn, who was still in Acapulco on an archaeological expedition.

'How are you, Dawn? And how are you getting on in Mexico?' asked Baguda, who was pleased to hear his sister's voice.

'I'm doing fine. I'm really enjoying my work here, but we'll be finishing in a few days time. My supervisor is really nice and we've discovered something new too,' said Dawn.

'What's the new discovery?'

'It's the fossilized remains of an extinct animal, which was thought to belong to the Mesozoic era, about 250 million years ago.'

'That's interesting. There's been another archaeological discovery in York. It was in the news today.'

'That's marvellous. How's Anonsa?'

'She's doing fine. She just left the sitting room.'

'Send my regards to her. It's a shame I haven't met her yet.'

'I will do. I wish you a safe journey back to the UK.'

'Thank you. I'll see you when I come back. Goodbye.'

'Goodbye and enjoy yourself,' said Baguda. After his conversation with his sister, Baguda went back to finishing his work. Meanwhile, Anonsa was upstairs on the phone chatting to one of her friends. After about an hour she joined him in the sitting room.

8

May 2003

Emily and Burnty were in the car heading home after a shopping expedition at The Shires Shopping Centre, in Leicester. It was several weeks after Burnty had been discharged from the hospital. He and Emily had managed to attend Chloe's swimming competition, which she won. Astrid and Nigel had been very excited when they turned up at the event, and so was Chloe. In Emily and Burnty's shopping bags there was a gift for Chloe, which they had promised her before the competition. There were also things for a party which was being organized by their friends to celebrate Burnty's recovery from his near-fatal accident. Many people had been invited to the party including Burnty's friend, Azuchukwu, who insisted on travelling from Nigeria for the party. Burnty's younger brother, Robert, also promised to come over from the USA. When they arrived home half an hour later Emily parked the car in the garage and they unloaded their shopping and carried it inside the house.

'What time are you due to attend the meeting at your club?' asked Burnty, as he lay stretched out on the sofa as though he had just had a fight with a sumo wrestler.

'Oh! Do you mean the Philatelic Club?'

'Yes.'

'I might have to phone them to tell them that I won't be able to attend today's meeting unfortunately. The venue has been moved to the Town Hall. I hope to be able to attend the one next month.'

She made a dash for the telephone. After phoning the club, she came back to join Burnty on the sofa. 'Somehow, philately does not interest me. I don't know why,' said Burnty.

'It's a strange hobby, but I usually find it very exciting for reasons that I can't really explain. I've been involved with philately since I was in school, because we used to have a philatelic club. Some of my classmates who knew about King George V's interest in philately nicknamed me "Georgina" and "Queen George V",' said Emily. 'The teacher who used to run the club was very well-informed about philatelic issues and he had an extraordinary collection of stamps from various countries of the world.'

'Was King George V really a philatelist?'

'Yes. Before he died, he was a very keen and well-known philatelist with a gargantuan collection of stamps,' Emily sounded deliberately grandiloquent.

'That's interesting. I thought it was only horses and polo that the British kings were interested in.'

'And of course women,' said Emily.

'Really?' Burnty looked surprised.

'I know that you haven't read much about British royalty. Have you heard about King Edward VII's exploits?'

'What do you mean?'

'I mean the number of women he slept with while he was Prince of Wales?'

'No, I haven't heard about that,' said Burnty. 'I'm aware of the "second-son syndrome" that Royal historians often refer to when talking about King George V and King George VI. But my knowledge in this respect is superficial.'

'Alright, let me enlighten you about royal history. It's fun to be able to play the historian, even with my own scanty area of knowledge,' said Emily. 'King Edward VII's eldest son was Albert Victor, who was supposed to become King, but he died in his late twenties when he was suddenly taken ill. That's how his younger brother eventually became King George V after the death of King Edward VII. He married Princess Mary of Teck, later Queen Mary, who had originally been engaged to Albert Victor, at the Chapel Royal in St James's Palace in London. History was to repeat itself, though in a different way, when King Edward VIII who succeeded his father, King George V, abdicated the throne and insisted on marrying an American divorcée by the name of Wallis Simpson. His younger brother, who was next in line, became King George VI and he was the father of our own Queen, Elizabeth II.' Emily looked triumphant when she had finished.

'Wasn't that a very risky thing to do? What if Wallis Simpson had abandoned him for another man, after he had given up everything for her?' said Burnty, who was listening attentively to Emily like a schoolboy on his first day at school.

'That's true. I suppose he never really believed that he wouldn't be allowed to marry her. If he had known that unequivocally, he might have seriously reconsidered his options. According to him, his real need was for happiness, but unfortunately he found that happiness in a woman who was not acceptable to the establishment.'

'Had he found the happiness he craved in a woman who *was* acceptable, do you think the result might have been different?'

'I suppose so, considering the fact that he was said to have been good at his job while he was Prince of Wales and also when he became king. He was remarkably popular, but his overwhelming desire for happiness, which he claimed he was deprived of by virtue of his upbringing, unfortunately clouded his sense of devotion to duty,' said Emily sadly.

'You seem to be quite sympathetic towards him?'

'Yes, you are quite right. It's because I've always tried to see all the sides to the story surrounding the issue of his abdication and the consequent constitutional upheaval that it provoked.'

'I think this has now been rectified and the House of Windsor has put the crisis behind it,' said Burnty.

'Yes, I agree with you.'

'There seem to be so many royal houses in British history. I've heard of the Stuarts, Tudors, York and Hanover. It's so confusing.'

'You're right. The name of Windsor actually came about during the reign of King George V, Queen Elizabeth II's grandfather. He changed the family name from Saxe-Coburg-Gotha to Windsor after the outbreak of the First World War, because it was a German name. Considering the understandable hostility of the British public to Germany during the war, I guess he felt compelled to do so. The rights and wrongs of it are better left to historians.'

'That's quite a mouthful of a name – Saxe-Coburg-Gotha,' said Burnty jocularly.

'That was where Queen Victoria's husband, Prince Albert came from,' said Emily, as they both flipped through the latest issue of the *Gardener* magazine.

They found a page which showed a picture of Casiraghi Romano, and as soon as Emily saw it she exclaimed, 'This is Astrid's father!' Emily looked excited.

'I was going to ask you about it when I saw the name, because I remember that you once told me Astrid's maiden name was Romano,' said Burnty.

'Her father was a renowned landscape gardener in the UK and Europe before he retired. He was said to have visited over a thousand major gardens all over the world as sources of inspiration for his works, including the gardens at Hampton Court Palace, where Henry VIII lived.'

'Wasn't Hampton Court Palace the venue of an EU Leaders' meeting a while ago?'

'Yes. You're right.'

'I saw the garden on TV, it was stunning. I think we should visit it one of these days.'

'That'd be lovely. My parents took us there when I was very young, but I don't remember it very well. Mum was pregnant with Lala at the time.'

'A repeat visit should help to refresh your memory. What a long discussion we've had about the British monarchy! I'm now filled with new knowledge about it all, thanks to your erudition.'

Burnty proceeded to plant a kiss on her lips and Emily responded like a weakly burning flame which suddenly had a jar of gasoline poured on it. Within minutes, they were both naked in the bedroom and they made love like two hungry wolves until they were both exhausted.

Emily and Burnty woke up very late in the morning. Being a Saturday, and the last weekend before Burnty returned to work, they had both vowed to make the most of it before they got sucked into their busy schedules in the hospital. It was Burnty who got out of bed first and he went downstairs to pick up the mail that had arrived for both of them. He took all the letters upstairs and handed Emily's letters to her. The first one Emily opened was from her club, the Leicester Philatelic Club which informed her that during their last meeting she had unanimously been elected, in absentia, as the President of the Club for the next year. If she accepted the offer, she would be entitled to free accommodation, meals and laundry for a week at a time at Churchill College, Cambridge, to enable her to learn more about philately. She could do this up to three times during her one year tenure. This had been part of the perks of the office of President for over thirty years, since the founding of the club. Emily was asked to fill in and return the letter of acceptance which was included in the envelope within seven days.

Emily was surprised and immensely overjoyed by the news. She immediately filled in the letter accepting the offer and agreeing to its terms and conditions. After sealing the envelope she put it to one side for posting the following day. Burnty congratulated her and proceeded to open his own mail.

The first letter he opened was confirming the date of his Advanced Trauma Life Support Course, the next contained tickets which he had ordered for them a few days earlier, for an exhibition at the New Walk Museum & Art Gallery, close to Waterloo Way. He put the tickets in a drawer and went into the study to reply to an email one of his friends had sent earlier in the week. Emily got dressed for her visit to see Clara, her beautician.

'Burnty, I'm off to the hairdressers,' said Emily, as she came out of the bedroom.

'Isn't that one of your letters lying there underneath the desk?' Burnty asked, pointing towards it.

Emily stopped and went to pick up the letter, which she must have dropped. She ripped open the brown manila envelope and took out the letter.

'Oh my goodness! Burnty, this is the letter I've been waiting for. I'm really thrilled.' She was ecstatic, and placed her left hand firmly on her chest as if to control her racing heart.

'Is it the one from Australia?'

'Yes, it is. It's the hospital in Sydney. They've granted my application for a two-month rotation in neonatology, and they say that I can go any time from now onwards.'

She then handed the letter to Burnty. After reading it, Burnty hugged her and said, 'This could be a marvellous opportunity for a reconciliation between you and your dad.'

'You're right! My dad has been desperate for us to meet for ages. We've been granted a rare opportunity and I'm sure we'll seize it with both hands. This is absolutely wonderful. I had been optimistic about the hospital in Adelaide, and now it's the one in Sydney, which I actually preferred, that has given me an offer.' Emily was clearly delighted.

She finally left the house and drove to the beauty salon. On the way she began to think of what her father's reaction would be when he found out about her impending trip to Sydney. She had never met her stepmother, though they had spoken on the phone on several occasions. Emily knew that she was from Brisbane and that her father was her first husband. Although she was eager to meet her father after such a long time, she was anxious about his cold attitude towards her relationship with Burnty. She had tried her best not to let Burnty know that her father was totally against them marrying. Her father had a near pathological aversion to foreigners, even those of the same racial stock as himself, and an almost hysterical loathing for people of other races. She loved Burnty and would really like to marry him, but she also craved a reconciliation with her father. Her father loved and cared about her, but they had always disagreed about her boyfriends.

She tried to take her mind off this as she negotiated the bend leading to the street where the beauty salon was located. When she arrived at the salon, there was only one other client so she was soon being seen by Clara, her favourite hairdresser and beautician.

Meanwhile, Burnty was sitting at home watching the TV. The Sky Movies Channel was showing *The Terminal,* and being based on an airport it suddenly occurred to him that he and Emily had not gone on holiday together for over a year. Their last holiday was in the Czech Republic and Slovakia. He thought that it would be a good idea to go somewhere else soon. His mind wandered to Asia and the Far East, and even to South America, but finally settled on Europe. He thought of Tuscany and got up to fetch the map of Europe from the bookcase. As he was opening the bookcase, the phone rang and he dashed to pick up the receiver.

'Hello, this is Burnty. Who's on the line?'

'Burnty, how are you? It's your daddy, calling from Nigeria,' came his father's voice.

'Ah, daddy! How nice to hear your voice. I hope you are doing well? How's mummy?'

'I'm alright my son. Your mummy is well too. She's gone to visit her friend. I hope you've regained your strength by now?'

'Yes, daddy. I'm even going back to work again on Monday.'

'Why so soon?' His father sounded surprised.

'That's the way it is here. I've actually been off work for some weeks now.'

'Really? It seems as though you've only been off for a week or so. How time flies! My prayers and thoughts are with you at all times. May you continue to climb higher and higher on the ladder of success. Your efforts will never be in vain and they will always end in success. By God's grace your marriage will be successful too. This is my prayer for all my children. Thank you for your recent financial gift. God will kindly reward you.' His father's voice was heavy with emotion.

'Thank you very much, daddy. I'm lucky to have both you and mummy as my parents.'

'How's your girlfriend?'

'She's doing fine too. She's gone to the hairdresser's to get her hair done.'

'You know that I've always advised you that it's the person that matters and not the colour of their skin. Take care of yourself. God will continue to protect you. I hope you are still attending church whenever you are not on hospital duty?'

'I'm trying my best, daddy. Send my greetings to mummy.'

'I'll do that,' said his father and the line went dead.

Burnty was exhilarated to have spoken to his father. They had spoken to each other several times since his accident. He only allowed Robert, his younger brother, to tell his parents what had happened after he had been safely discharged from the hospital. As he had anticipated, his parents had been very worried when they heard about it. His mother could not eat for twenty-four hours after she heard the news and she insisted that they should visit him in the UK. Burnty had managed to dissuade them, since he was already out of hospital and recuperating.

After the conversation with his father, Burnty went back to the bookcase, got out the map of Europe and sat on the sofa.

He had just located Tuscany when the phone started ringing again. He went reluctantly to pick up the receiver.

'Hello, this is Burnty Christopher. Who's on the line please?' His voice was formal.

'Hi Burnty. It's Dominic calling from Rangoon in Myanmar.'

'Dominic, how are you and how was the competition?' Burnty lit up with excitement.

'I just phoned to tell you that I won! I came first and I've been given the task to sculpt the statue of U Thant, the former UN Secretary-General,' said Dominic, who sounded as though he was struggling to hold back his tears.

'Congratulations! I trust your talent and I know how good you are, but I must say that I'm completely delighted for you to have succeeded on such an astonishingly huge scale,' said Burnty, who was completely bowled over and almost shaking with emotion. 'How about the ceremony?'

'It was held soon after the announcement. I was so surprised that I broke down in tears. You are the first person I've told. I've been crying since I was announced as the winner. I haven't even told Isabel yet. She's heavily pregnant and I don't want her to get overly excited. I'll only tell her when I arrive back in the UK tomorrow.'

'I think we need to celebrate this. This award will transform you into an internationally acclaimed sculptor. I think that we should incorporate a celebration for your award into the party which has been planned to celebrate my recovery, we can't let something this momentous pass by unrecognized.'

'Thank you. That's a great idea. I've got an interview with one of the TV stations here in Rangoon, so I'll be leaving my hotel soon.'

'Which hotel are you staying in?'

'It's the Renaissance Inya Lake Hotel, on Kaba Aye Pagoda Road.'

'Alright, we'd better round up our conversation. Have a nice interview and I wish you a safe journey back. We'll speak again when you arrive in the UK.'

'Thank you,' said Dominic and the line went dead.

After hanging up, Dominic went down to the hotel bar and ordered a glass of red wine. He began to think about the whirlwind of activities that had taken place in the last twenty-four hours. He had become a mini-celebrity in Rangoon overnight and had been interviewed by journalists from all the major newspapers, who all seemed to ask similar questions. His next interview was the first by a TV network, but he was well prepared for it.

He had broken down in tears after he was announced as the winner of the competition. While giving his speech, he had thanked the organizers, UNESCO, for giving him the opportunity to showcase his talents to the world. He had dedicated the award to his parents and his late aunt and uncle, who had looked after him when his mother died. He had eulogized over their efforts and the immense contribution they had made towards his success in life.

Dominic finished his drink and boarded the taxi which was waiting to take him to the TV station.

After speaking to Dominic, Burnty went into the kitchen and made a cup of coffee for himself. He was overjoyed at the news of Dominic's success at the UNESCO Competition. He knew that his cousin was very talented but, winning this competition was a powerful and indubitable validation of his artistic prowess. He wished him well and looked forward to seeing him in the UK. Burnty was dozing off to sleep on the sofa when Emily arrived back, waking him up.

'Don't tell me that you are sleeping already?' joked Emily, as she breezed into the lounge looking radiant with her new hairstyle.

'H'm! You look gorgeous,' Burnty complimented her. He got up to kiss her and stroke her hair.

'It's all for you so I'm glad that you like it,' Emily smiled.

'You're my one and only, to adore and love from the depths of my heart.'

'Thank you. Let's keep our love as constant as the Northern star.'

'I've got news for you.'

'What news?'

'Dominic has won the UNESCO Sculpture Competition in Myanmar. He phoned to tell me a while ago.'

'How marvellous! He must be very talented.'

'Even he was surprised by the outcome. He's flying back to the UK tomorrow.'

'That's great. He'll want to celebrate. Why not incorporate the celebration into your party?'

'You must have read my mind! I already suggested that and he was thrilled with the idea.'

'That's fantastic.'

'When are you planning to go to Australia?'

'It'll have to be after your party. I'll also need to speak to my supervising consultant at the Royal Infirmary and to the paediatric department in the hospital in Sydney.'

Emily and Burnty settled down to enjoy the rest of their quiet afternoon with a game of scrabble and some soft music on the CD player.

It was over two weeks since Emily had been elected as the new President of the Philatelic Club, and she was driving towards the Town Hall where she had called a members' meeting. She was looking forward to presiding over the meeting and also seeing Richard again. By sheer coincidence, Richard was also a member of the Philatelic Club. He had joined the club before Emily. He was present at the meeting where Emily was elected President and he was looking forward to seeing her again. They had not seen each other since their one-night stand many months before.

He had been going out with a new girlfriend, who was a ballet dancer, and had also been very busy with his business commitments all over the UK. He had thought about Emily from time to time, especially when he drove past the Royal Infirmary.

Emily was now in front of the Town Hall so she parked her car and walked briskly inside. The meeting was scheduled for 2.15 p.m. and she had arrived about fifteen minutes early. Richard was already there waiting for her. He had been elected as Treasurer of the club. There were fifty-one members of the club, but most of them attended its social events rather than its meetings. There were only five other members, apart from Richard, waiting in the room when Emily entered. Everyone seemed to be happy to see her and shouted out their congratulations. She said, 'thank you everyone,' and proceeded to greet each of them in turn, hugging them and shaking hands. She gave Richard a particularly big hug and then took her seat beside him. She congratulated him on his re-election as the Treasurer and they began to chat together. Within ten minutes more people had arrived and by the time the meeting started there were thirty-seven members in the room.

'This is just amazing! Thirty-seven people present at the meeting? I can't believe it,' said one of the members, who looked delighted.

'It must be due to the Emily factor,' someone shouted out. Emily blushed with embarrassment.

She was well liked by the members and quite popular among them, a fact that was all too obvious by her unanimous election. She was a gregarious and warm hearted person, unassuming and with a keen sense of humour. People found her easy to get along with. Emily started the meeting by formally thanking everyone for the confidence they had reposed in her. She promised to serve the club to the best of her ability. After her short, impromptu speech, she was given a standing ovation. During the meeting they went through all the items on the agenda and reviewed the future activities of the club. Emily's predecessor, Dudley Schwartz, a fifty-five-year-old school teacher, formally handed over his files and went on to describe the new arrangements for the residential course at Churchill College, Cambridge.

Emily noted these down. She was also told the date for the next residential course, which would be her first. Luckily it was still far away. The meeting ended on a pleasant note and everyone left after having some light refreshments.

Emily and Richard seemed to have re-ignited the spark of their affair again, as they were virtually inseparable after the meeting had ended. She wrote Richard's telephone number on a piece of paper but deliberately didn't store it in her cell phone for fear that Burnty might find out. Richard immediately entered her number into the address book of his cell phone. However, they agreed not to phone each other in order to avoid detection. They intended using the executive meetings, which had only eight members, as a smokescreen for their clandestine affair. They finally parted and each of them got into their respective cars and drove away.

Emily headed home, stopping on the way to buy some groceries in a roadside shop. When she arrived home, she parked the car and headed towards the front door. As she fumbled for her house keys, it suddenly dawned on her that she had left them inside. Burnty was on on-call duty at the hospital, so Emily phoned to tell him that she was on her way to collect the house keys from him. She arrived at the hospital and collected the keys from Burnty and drove back home. As soon as she got inside the house she kicked off her shoes, removed her clothes and hopped into the shower. She came out feeling refreshed. After getting dressed again, she went into the kitchen and poured herself a glass of orange juice, then went to sit in the lounge. She plugged in her laptop and began to surf the internet.

She was looking for a hotel in Sydney in preparation for her impending trip to Australia. She had decided that she'd start by staying in a hotel and then find out if it would be convenient for her to stay with her father and his family. She was a bit wary of her step-mother whom she had never met. She also looked at the British Medical Journal Careers website to find out what consultant posts in paediatrics were available. She did this from time to time out of curiosity, since one day she'd become a consultant paediatrician. After disconnecting her laptop, she began to mull over many things. Her mind went to Burnty, who had yet to obtain a specialist registrar post in spite of having attended lots of interviews. She also thought of one of her former classmates in Leicester, who was now a consultant paediatrician in a hospital in Philadelphia. She thought about her sisters, especially Lala whose career as an actress had soared to a level that nobody had expected. Finally Emily switched on the TV and went to remove some food from the freezer in the kitchen, as she wanted to prepare a meal for Burnty when he got back that evening.

She sat down to watch the TV, occasionally going into the kitchen to check on her cooking. When the programme she was watching finished, Emily switched to SkySports which was showing the previous UEFA Champions League matches. The match that was being shown was Arsenal v Real Madrid, to be followed by Manchester United v AC Milan. Emily enjoyed watching the football even though she was more of a tennis fan. She had been to some Wimbledon Finals in the past, where the winners of the Men's and Women's Singles titles were presented with their trophies by the Duke of Kent. She poured herself more orange juice and continued watching the match. Emily was pleased to have seen Richard again, though she found it difficult to reconcile the emotional ambivalence that engulfed her. On the one hand, she loved and adored Burnty, yet after she slept with Richard she had felt a mixture of guilt and satisfaction. She began to wonder whether this had anything to do with her father's disapproval of her relationship with Burnty and her subconscious desire to please him. She could not fully understand her own emotions. But one thing was clear: she wanted to be surrounded by love. She was loved by two men in her life, but she wanted it unconditionally from a third man – her father. She knew that her mother and sisters loved her very much.

After a while, Emily got up and looked out of the window. She saw a group of children who were playing in a nearby house and she started imagining what it would be like to have her own children. She enjoyed working with children, which was why she had chosen to work in paediatrics. She went into the kitchen to check on the meal as Burnty was due home shortly. As she stood in the kitchen her elbow hit a pile of china plates and they came tumbling down on the floor. A few of them were completely smashed. She grimaced as she cleared the debris from the floor. She had barely finished doing that when the doorbell rang. She put down the fragments of broken plate and went to open the door. On opening the door, she saw Burnty standing there looking drawn and tired.

'Hi darling, you look worn out,' said Emily, as she rushed to embrace him.

'I've literally been on my feet since this morning. I was in theatre for many hours and had no time to eat anything. I'm really famished.'

Burnty collapsed onto the sofa and stretched out his legs while Emily went into the kitchen to collect the food. Burnty then joined her in the dining room and they ate together. When they finished their meal they went back to the sitting room, where the TV was still showing the match between Manchester United v AC Milan. As soon as Burnty saw it he lit up like a giant chandelier in a dark room. 'It's as if all the patients I was supposed to have seen while I was off sick were waiting for me. Since I went back to work they've been pouring in like an avalanche, on a scale I hadn't seen before since I joined this hospital.'

'It's been really quiet for me in the paediatrics department. The last time I experienced that volume of work was when I was a senior house officer, before I got the specialist registrar job. I suppose it's busy in paediatrics department too, but because the senior house officers see and sort out many of the patients, they never really get referred to me. But I'm sure you'll cope as you've always done in the past.'

'Thanks, for your constant support darling. Do you know when the Liverpool v Ajax match is scheduled for?'

'We'll have to check that. They've already shown the match between *Arsenal v Real Madrid.*'

'I just hope that I won't be as busy during the next World Cup event.'

'Am I right in thinking Brazil are the defending champions, after winning the Cup in 2002?'

'That's right.'

'This four-yearly event has been going on for over a hundred years now and the passion for it has consumed the world like a huge ball of flame.'

'I quite agree with you, but it's not a hundred years since the FIFA World Cup started,' Burnty corrected her.

'Really? I always thought that it was as old as the modern Olympics. Anyhow, at least it's good to be able to watch it.'

'The first FIFA World Cup tournament was held in 1930 in Uruguay, who won it.'

'It seems that the host country has a tendency to win.'

'Not always. Since 1930, when it was first held, host countries have only won the cup on five occasions: in 1934, Italy hosted and won it; so did England in 1966; and then West Germany did in 1974. It happened again in Argentina in 1978 and there was a twenty-year gap until 1998, when France hosted and won it,' said Burnty looking pleased.

'That's impressive. I know that you're a football buff.'

'Well, it's a big hobby of mine. We swap positions of knowledge from time to time. I'm a teacher of FIFA World Cup history today, after being a student of British history under your tutelage.'

'H'm, we must be soul mates. It's such a delight to always be able to discuss and debate things between ourselves, and yet be able to see each other's point of view,' said Emily, and she proceeded to kiss Burnty.

'I'm lucky to be with such a witty, understanding and analytical person like you.'

'I think we're both lucky in that respect.'

'I know that there is a football competition held in Africa just like the World Cup event, but I don't know what it's called,' said Emily looking uncertain.

'It's called the African Nations Cup and is held every four years.'

'How has Nigeria fared in the events?'

'Since it was first held in 1957 in Sudan, Nigeria has won it on two occasions. Firstly, in 1980 and secondly, in 1994. Nigeria also made it to three of the Finals in 1988, 1990 and 2000.'

'Wouldn't it be great if you could run a football academy with your impressive knowledge of football?'

'Thank you, but I haven't finished yet. Nigeria also won the Olympic gold medal in football in 1996 in Atlanta, USA.'

'That's remarkable.'

'Now that we've talked about football, let's talk about where we'll go for our next holiday. I've been thinking of Tuscany and Milan. What do you think?'

'I've been to Tuscany before so let's try Milan. We can go there when I get back from Australia.'

'That's fine with me. I think your mum intends to visit the UK after your Australian trip.'

'Yes. She'll be around for a while. She's coming to help Helen with her baby and her husband will be in the UK at the same time due to work commitments.'

'What about your philately course at Churchill College? When is that coming up?'

'It's much later in the year. I'll have plenty of time after my return from Australia before it starts. I'm really looking forward to it. My predecessor told me that he really enjoyed it.'

'It's nice to hear that, and it should also help to enrich your knowledge of philately from around the world.'

'That's very true.'

9

June 2003

Dominic arrived at Heathrow with joy and enthusiasm as he looked forward to being reunited with his pregnant wife, Isabel. After collecting his luggage he walked out of the terminal towards the taxi rank. There had been a heavy rainfall just before his flight arrived, so when he went outside he was taken aback by the continued heavy rainfall. He already missed the warm temperatures in Rangoon, which he had only left behind about twenty-four hours ago. He went back inside the terminal and bought a cup of coffee at Caffè Nero. As he ordered it, he spotted an acquaintance whom he had said goodbye to earlier on after they had both collected their luggage. He was sitting at one of the nearby tables, sipping coffee and reading one of the local newspapers. His name was McAlistar Syke, and he was a veterinary surgeon from Hull. He had been living in Rangoon for over twenty years with his Nigerian wife and four children. He had come back to the UK to visit his parents and had been sitting next to Dominic on the plane. He saw Dominic queuing up to buy coffee and said, 'Hi Dominic, are you still here?'

'Yes. I went outside to get a taxi, and got a blast of wind right on my face. Suddenly I realized I hadn't told my wife that I had arrived and was on my way, so I decided to do that over a cup of coffee. You are still here too?'

'Yes, I'm waiting for a friend of mine who's supposed to pick me up. I didn't really ask what you were doing in Rangoon. I know that you are an artist with the Tate Modern.'

'I went for a UNESCO International Competition for Artists and I won it.' Dominic now had a cup of coffee in his hands and he joined McAlistar at his table.

'Was it the competition for the erection of the statue of U Thant, the former UN Secretary-General?'

'Yes, that was it. So you knew about it?' Dominic looked surprised.

'Oh yes! I knew all about it and also that it had been won by a UK-based Nigerian sculptor. My wife, who's Nigerian, and I had discussed it. So it was you? How marvellous. There I was sitting beside a celebrity sculptor without even knowing it. I'll let my wife know about it when I return to Rangoon, she'll be so delighted. Accept my congratulations.'

'Thank you. It was a very tedious week for me. I was completely surprised when I was announced as the winner.'

Dominic dialled his home telephone number to tell Isabel that he had arrived in London and would soon be on his way home to join her and her mother, Jeanette, who had come from Germany to stay with her. Isabel was ecstatic when she picked up the phone and learnt of Dominic's arrival. As they spoke, he broke the news to her that he had won the competition. On hearing this, she was overcome with emotion and broke down in tears of joy. She was absolutely thrilled by the news, which she quickly relayed to her mother who was busy in the kitchen.

After finishing his conversation with Isabel, Dominic drank the last of his coffee and shook hands with McAlistar. They exchanged telephone numbers and e-mail addresses before he eventually left. On the way home he peered through the taxi window at a tree-lined road that reminded him of Rangoon. He was happy to be back in London. He felt exhausted after the long flight and he dozed off intermittently. In slightly less than an hour, he arrived home.

Isabel promptly answered the door when he rang the doorbell. She rushed to embrace him and planted passionate kisses on his lips and cheeks. Tears began to roll down her face while her mother watched them in approval. As they finally loosened their embrace, Isabel muttered, 'Congratulations, darling. I simply don't know what to say. I'm over the moon.'

'Thank you, honey,' Dominic managed to say as he broke down in tears himself, remembering his mother and his aunt and uncle, who were all dead. They were both comforted by Isabel's mother, Jeanette, who was equally moved by the emotional spectacle before her. She went to fetch some tissues for them to dry their eyes.

'Welcome back and congratulations, my son,' said Jeanette, as Dominic and Isabel sat down together on the sofa.

'Thank you, mummy,' said Dominic.

'I didn't ever imagine you had won, since you didn't mention anything about it when you last spoke to me from Rangoon. I presumed that someone else must have won the competition,' said Isabel.

'I didn't want you to get overly excited while I was away especially now that you are approaching the term of your pregnancy. That's why I kept the news until the last minute,' said Dominic as he stroked her swollen abdomen.

'There'll be absolute pandemonium in the office tomorrow when they get to know about it. I haven't been in the office for three days now but I knew everyone's been itching to find out the outcome of the competition. I'm sure the boss will already know by now, since it's over twenty-four hours since it was announced. He's been keeping tabs on the event. You know what he's like, he'll want you to get in bright and early tomorrow.'

'I'm almost sure that he knows the result already as he's been closely monitoring it. Since we'll both be going to the office together tomorrow, we'll both find out what they have in store for me. Today is the beginning of the month and tomorrow is your last day before the start of your maternity leave, isn't it?'

'That's right. You must be very tired now,' said Isabel as Dominic began to doze off to sleep. She nudged him on the shoulder and he sat upright momentarily before kicking off his shoes and socks and heading to bed.

Dominic was woken in the middle of the night by Isabel's cries. He had been asleep for over eight hours when Isabel suddenly went into labour. She was having painful contractions and her mother was with her. Dominic quickly phoned for an ambulance which arrived very quickly and she was whisked off to the Queen Charlotte Hospital. Dominic and her mother both went with her.

On arriving in the labour ward, Isabel was seen by the senior house officer on duty, Dr Melibo Galverston, who diagnosed a breech presentation of one of the twins. An ultrasound scan had confirmed the presence of twins many weeks before, and this procedure was repeated on her arrival at the hospital. Isabel was admitted and her condition stabilized while Dr Galverston paged the consultant, for a further review of her case. Dominic, who was not comfortable in hospital environments looked panicky and distressed. He was remembering his visit to see his cousin, Burnty, in hospital in Leicester. But Dominic was reassured by the look on Jeanette's face. Jeanette was by Isabel's side and was comforting her. She had been through a similar and even worse experience herself when she gave birth to her own children. She had delivered her babies by Caesarian section twice. Not long afterwards, the consultant-on-duty, Mr Hermann Ulrich, a German obstetrician arrived to assess Isabel. After introducing himself and exchanging a few pleasantries, he proceeded to interview her about her medical history and examined her. Mr Ulrich noticed that she was not making progress in her labour, so decided she would have to have a Caesarian. He informed Isabel about this and obtained her consent before arrangements were made for her to be taken to the operating theatre. Isabel was looking calm, though she cried out whenever she had a painful contraction.

'You'll be alright. Just be strong,' said Jeanette.

'Darling, you'll be fine,' said Dominic, who was experiencing mixed emotions.

On the one hand he was delighted by his impending fatherhood but also frightened and worried about Isabel's condition. He prayed silently for the best outcome for her and the babies.

Shortly afterwards, porters arrived to take Isabel to the operating theatre, and she was accompanied by one of the midwives who were looking after her. Shortly afterwards she was delivered of a boy and a girl. The female twin looked stronger and cried briskly but the male twin was smaller and his skin had a bluish tinge. He was promptly transferred to the Neonatal Intensive Care Unit, to be looked after by the paediatricians, while Isabel was transferred to the ward with the female twin, for post-operative care. She was kept well informed about the condition of her son.

Dominic was overjoyed when Isabel was wheeled back into the ward.

'Congratulations, to both of you, new parents,' teased Jeanette while she stroked Isabel's hair.

'Thank you, mummy,' said Isabel and Dominic together.

Isabel lay in her hospital bed, occasionally grimacing in pain. It was about 4 a.m. in the morning, and Dominic had to go to work later in the day. Soon afterwards Isabel was assessed by Mr Ulrich and his team of junior doctors. Dominic spoke to Mr Ulrich and asked how long his wife was likely to have to stay in hospital. After making sure that everything was under control, Dominic went back home to prepare for work, while Jeanette remained with Isabel.

Dominic arrived at his office to a tumultuous welcome by his colleagues. His boss, Drian Huskett, was immensely proud of his achievement. As Dominic had guessed, he had been monitoring the event on the internet. Dominic was given light duties for the early part of the day and an office cocktail party was organized in the afternoon in his honour. Dominic started work after breaking the news of his wife's delivery of a son and daughter. He also telephoned Burnty, who was at home and off duty after a week of working nights.

'Hello, Burnty,' said Dominic when the call went through.

'Hi Dominic. I've been waiting for your call. I phoned your house last night, but there was no response and your cell phone and Isabel's were both switched off. I was slightly worried. How are you? Welcome back to the UK.'

'Thank you. We weren't at home when you phoned. Isabel suddenly went into labour in the middle of the night and she had to be rushed to Queen Charlotte Hospital. She delivered twin babies by Caesarian section last night.'

'You can't be serious! I hope she's in a stable condition. It did not even cross my mind at all. I thought she wasn't due for another two weeks?'

'Yes, you're right. It all happened earlier than we expected. Thank God she is in a stable condition as so is the female twin, but the male twin is still in the Neonatal Intensive Care Unit.'

'So they are of mixed sex?'

'Yes.'

'How's your daughter doing?'

'She's alright. She's already suckling her mother's breasts.'

'I'll come and visit them this weekend, since I'm free until next week. Let me have the phone number of her ward.'

Dominic searched through the phone list in his cell phone and read out the number to Burnty.

'We've been making arrangements for the party but it'll have to wait until Isabel is discharged from hospital.'

'That's very kind of you. They've planned a small cocktail party for me this afternoon in the office. Everybody was delighted with the news.'

'That's great. I really hope that this will be the beginning of greater things for you.

'Thank you.'

'So you've plunged back into work already?'

'Well, I couldn't wait to come back to work, even though my boss has given me light duties for today. I thought that you'd be at work today. I just decided to try my luck by phoning your house first. How's your work going?'

'I just finished a week of night duty, so I'm off for a few days.'

'How's Emily doing?'

'She's doing fine. She's working today. After the party, she'll be going to Australia for two months.'

'Whereabouts in Australia?'

'Sydney, which, coincidentally is where her father lives with his second wife and their kids. She's very happy at the prospect of being with her father again.'

'It sounds exciting.'

'I'm so relieved now that we have spoken to each other and I know what's going on with you and Isabel.'

'That's good.'

'How about Isabel's mother? Is she still with her?'

'Yes, she is. We were so lucky that Jeanette was there. She stayed with Isabel in the hospital when I left for work. I can't even imagine how I would have coped had her mother been not around.'

'That's very lucky. As I said, I'll come to London this weekend. If Emily is free, we might even come together as she's been itching to see Isabel. I'll leave you to prepare for your cocktail party now and I'll call before we come to London.'

'Thank you and goodbye.'

'Enjoy yourself and take care,' said Burnty and the line went dead.

Dominic was delighted to have shared the news about his wife and the babies with Burnty. He always appreciated the emotional and psychological support his cousin gave him whenever he was in distress. It really helped to calm him down. Dominic sipped coffee while he went through the files lying on his desk. Even though he had been given light duties for the day, he ended up clearing the backlog of work that had accumulated in his absence.

Dominic left the office early after the cocktail party and phoned Isabel in the hospital, before going home. He ate a light meal, had a shower and changed into a pair of jeans and a T-shirt before driving straight to the hospital. He arrived at the ward carrying a bag with the items Isabel had asked him to bring along. Meanwhile, Jeanette had gone to the Neonatal Intensive Care Unit to see her grandson, who was still in a critical condition. After exchanging greetings with the nurses, Dominic walked into Isabel's room.

'Hi, honey. You look great! How are you feeling?' asked Dominic.

'Hi, darling, it's nice to see you back so soon. I'm feeling good and our daughter is in excellent condition, but her brother's still in bad shape.'

'Where's mummy?'

'She's gone to see him.'

After kissing his daughter, whose name they hadn't decided on yet, Dominic went to see his son. He met his mother-in-law there. After speaking with the nurses he was led to the baby's cot. Dominic was clearly distraught by the baby's condition. He was struggling to hold back tears and he had to be comforted by the nurses. He then went into the visitors' lounge to join Jeanette and they both talked about the baby's condition, after which they went together to Isabel's ward.

'Did you bring my other make-up box?' asked Isabel, as Dominic and Jeanette entered the room.

Dominic could not answer her question as he was still thinking about his son. Isabel had cried all day when she was informed about the baby's worsening condition and she was now calm. She began to search the bag that Dominic had brought for her and she eventually found the box she was looking for. Dominic sat in the chair looking pensive and with his head bowed.

'Did I bring everything you asked for?' said Dominic in a weak and almost inaudible voice, while Jeanette looked on sympathetically.

'Yes, thank you. I've been crying all day about the baby but now I've decided to leave everything in God's hands. I need to draw on my belief in God for strength and believe that all will be well. The doctors and nurses are definitely trying their hardest and in the circumstances, we can only hope for the best.'

Dominic managed to speak at last. 'I agree with your words. We can only hope for the best. How about the doctors who are looking after you? What did they say today?'

'You mean Mr Ulrich and his team?'

'Yes.'

'He's been here today. He checked my wound and said that he was happy with how it was healing. He also told me that the results of all my blood tests were normal and said that they'll continue to keep me under observation. Our daughter was also given the all clear by the paediatricians.'

'It's nice to hear that. It means that you may not be staying in hospital for long.'

'Well, I hope so. Do you know that Mr Ulrich, the consultant, was my elder brother's classmate at the University of Bonn?'

'Really? That's interesting.'

'He found out that I am German and we got talking and I told him that my elder brother was a gynaecologist in Munich. He then mentioned the names of some of the gynaecologists he knew in Munich, and he said my brother's name, Dr Jurgen Fritz. I was delighted. He then told me that they were classmates during their undergraduate days at the University and that they had completed their internship training together in the same hospital.'

'How marvellous. I didn't realize your brother attended Bonn University, I thought he went to Heidelberg.' Dominic was surprised.

'No, we both graduated from Bonn. He was the one who influenced my choice of university. My dad had felt that I should go to Munich or Heidelberg, but my brother persuaded him to allow me to go to Bonn. That was how I ended up there and I really loved it.'

'That's great.'

'My mum used to know Mr Ulrich's family, because my brother used to talk about him then, but she never met him. After they finished their internship, Jurgen and Mr Ulrich haven't seen each other again, because Mr Ulrich moved to the UK and my brother remained in Germany.'

'I was so happy when he mentioned that he knew my son,' said Jeanette who was suffused with a sense of pride.

'It's really nice to hear this. It's a small world,' said Dominic.

'By the way, how did it go in the office today?' asked Isabel.

'The cocktail party went well and I was able to speak to Burnty too. He promised to come and see us this weekend.'

'I've spoken to him already. He phoned me earlier in the day. I guess it must have been after you talked to him. Emily also phoned and we spoke at length. She told me that she may be coming to London with Burnty if her schedule permits, but she was not certain yet whether she would be free. She also mentioned Burnty's party and she said that they thought it would be best to leave it until after I've been discharged from the hospital.'

'You already know everything then. I was going to tell you all of that myself.'

'Mummy and I thought it was very kind of Emily and Burnty to postpone the party because of me. I was so delighted when Emily told me. I couldn't bear to miss it, especially when your success in Rangoon is also going to be celebrated.'

'It really is very kind of them, considering the fact that other guests will have to adjust their schedules too. Mr Huskett and your colleagues in the office said that I should send you their best.'

'That's very kind of them. Daddy phoned me today and said to tell you to check your e-mail as he'll be sending you a message. He was on his way to Ulm from Munich, where he went to visit my brother.'

'That's great. Thank you.'

'He's missing mummy terribly,' Isabel glanced at Jeanette and smiled, and her mother smiled back.

'Of course, what do you expect? I'm sure that mummy is missing him too,' said Dominic and all three of them burst into laughter.

'Don't mind Isabel. She's got a peculiar sense of humour,' said Jeanette, who was still laughing.

'That's why we get on so well with each other,' said Isabel.

10

Emily and Burnty were driving to the Jomansa Hotel in Leicester,
Emily was behind the wheel and they were chatting together
animatedly. This was the venue where the party to celebrate
Burnty's recovery and Dominic's triumph was to be held.

Burnty's younger brother, Robert, who had arrived from the
USA two days before, had gone ahead to the hotel to help co-
ordinate the event. Burnty's friend, Azuchukwu, had also arrived
from Nigeria. He had been staying in London with his uncle
and was travelling to Leicester for the event. Many other people
had also been invited, most of whom were members of staff
of the Royal Infirmary in Leicester, where Emily and Burnty
worked. It had been about three weeks since Isabel was
discharged from hospital. She had fully recovered from her
operation and her wound was healing nicely but unfortunately,
she had lost her son. The surviving female twin had been
named Ingrid, and Isabel would be coming to the party without
her. She was being left in the care of Jeanette, who was still
staying with Isabel and Dominic. Emily and Burnty eventually

arrived at the hotel and pulled up in the parking lot. They got out of the car looking resplendent in their chosen outfits. Emily was wearing a black, silk dress while Burnty had on a white, two-piece suit. They went into the hotel holding hands. On entering the hall, which was filled with decorated tables and chairs, Burnty spotted Azuchukwu who had already arrived. He walked up to him and they shook hands and hugged each other tightly. 'Welcome, Azu. I'm overjoyed that you've been able to make it. I hope your trip from London was smooth,' said Burnty.

'Yes, it was quite smooth, thank you. I'm so happy that I was able to make it too. We haven't seen each other for quite some time and I thought that this would be a good opportunity for us to meet again,' said Azuchukwu, while they still held on to each other's hands.

After Emily and Azuchukwu had greeted each other, she went to greet the other guests who had arrived, most of whom were their colleagues from the hospital. Then Emily joined Burnty and Azuchukwu and they all chatted together. Moments later, Dominic arrived with Isabel who went straight to hug Emily.

'Hi Isabel. It's so nice to see you. You're looking great! How's Ingrid?' asked Emily.

'Thank you. It's nice to see you too. Ingrid is doing fine. She's with my mum, who asked me to say hello to you and Burnty on her behalf. She was thrilled to see you, when you both came to visit me in the hospital.'

'Oh, it's nice to hear that,' said Emily. They were then joined by some friends. Robert, who had been elsewhere in the hotel came to meet the large number of people who had arrived, and as soon as he saw Azuchukwu, he rushed to embrace him and they shook hands warmly.

'How's your training going?' asked Azuchukwu.

'It's going on well, thank you, and how's your wife?'

'She's doing fine. It's just marvellous to be with both of you in the UK,' said Azuchukwu, as Dominic joined them.

Burnty introduced Dominic to Azuchukwu as they had never met before. Azuchukwu congratulated him on his success at the UNESCO-sponsored competition and they all continued to chat among themselves.

The hall was filling up now and there was classical music playing in the background. The Master of Ceremonies was Gobse Norono, a lecturer of biochemistry at St Andrew's University, who was Burnty's friend. After everyone was seated he stood up to speak and silence fell. He announced the reasons for the party and eulogized both Burnty and Dominic. He later proposed a toast to Burnty's good health. Soon the food, champagne and wine were served and the guests ate and drank to their hearts' delight. Robert looked happy and excited to be at the party. This was his first trip to visit Burnty in the UK since his residency training in the USA had begun.

Meanwhile, Burnty and Azuchukwu were busy reminiscing about their alma mater, the University of Lagos, while Dominic also reminisced about the Ahmadu Bello University in Zaria. Emily was not entirely cut off from the discussion either, as she was familiar with Lagos University Teaching Hospital, having done an elective rotation there when she was a medical student.

The atmosphere was very lively as the food and drinks flowed freely. After dinner was over, the hall was cleared of the tables and chairs so that everyone could dance. Burnty danced very enthusiastically, as if to compensate for the dancing he'd been deprived of at the Blueshaft Nightclub all those months before. The dancing continued until the early hours of the following morning, when the guests began to trickle out of the hall one after the other.

After the party was over Burnty drove himself, Emily and Azuchukwu home, since he had not been drinking. When all the other guests had left, Robert, Dominic and Isabel went together to Burnty's house by taxi. On the journey, the three of them talked about how much they had enjoyed their evening at the hotel. When they all got back to Burnty and Emily's house, they were so exhausted that they all went to bed soon afterwards.

Dominic and Isabel had not made love since Isabel was discharged from hospital, so as soon as they climbed into the spare room bed they went into a frenzied love-making session that drained them of all the passionate desires that had built up in their veins like ice crystals. They woke up much later in the day looking refreshed, and after showering together they got dressed and went downstairs. They were later joined by Azuchukwu, Robert, Emily and Burnty and they all sat around the dining table eating. After they had had their meal, Burnty drove Azuchukwu, Dominic and Isabel to the station where they boarded a train to London. Azuchukwu was travelling back to Nigeria the following evening.

By the time Burnty came back from the station Robert and Emily were asleep again. They wanted to have as much rest as possible, as they were both embarking on long journeys the following day. Robert was due to travel back to Baltimore, while Emily was going to Sydney to start her two-month clinical rotation in paediatrics at the Sydney Children's Hospital.

When Burnty got home he sat in the sitting room and switched on the TV. After a few hours Robert joined him.

'It's good that you are well rested before starting your long journey back to the USA,' said Burnty.

'It's so crucial, if I'm to enjoy my trip tomorrow. I have to go to Birmingham International Airport first and then fly to Heathrow from there.'

'We'll leave home in good time tomorrow.'

'I think Emily is travelling to Sydney tomorrow too?'

'Yes. But, she'll be flying direct from Manchester Airport, after catching a train from Leicester.'

'Mummy and daddy were delighted about the party and they both wished me a safe journey back to the USA.'

'That's what parents are there for: giving support in difficult times. We are lucky that they are still together.'

'I quite agree with you. The next thing they'll be anxious to see will be our weddings.'

'That'll happen when the time is ripe,' said Burnty.

Shortly afterwards Emily came downstairs rubbing her eyes.

'Honey, I hope that you are well rested?' said Burnty walking towards her and kissing her on the lips.

'Yes, thank you. Hi Robert, I hope you've enjoyed your time in Leicester?' said Emily as she joined them in the sitting room.

'Yes, thank you. It's been marvellous, and it's a shame that I have to leave so soon,' said Robert.

'It's just one of those things. I'm leaving for Australia tomorrow too and I'll be gone for two months,' said Emily.

'Poor Burnty, how's he going to cope?' said Robert.

'He's a stoic. I know that he'll cope well,' said Emily giggling.

'Did I hear the physician's bundle of sympathy drop on my head with a thud?' asked Burnty jocularly.

'There were actually two: one from the adult's physician and one from the children's physician. Open them carefully because you'll need them when we've both flown away tomorrow,' said Emily while they all burst out laughing.

'I'll do that,' said Burnty.

'What's the training like in the USA?' asked Emily.

'It's quite hectic, but I'm enjoying it and I'll soon be finishing my third year.'

'That's good,' said Emily.

'I spent a year in Princeton and my house was on Mercer Street. I remember that whenever I gave my address, I always got asked about Albert Einstein, the world-renowned physicist.'

'Really? Did he live in Princeton?' asked Emily looking astonished.

'Oh yes. I did not realize it myself, until I was told by an elderly lady who had known him when he lived on that street when she was a child.'

'That's interesting. I think we should call Burnty the Albert Einstein link! His younger brother lived on the same street as the famous man, and his cousin's wife was born in the same town as him,' said Emily.

'How about that, Burnty?' said Robert with a wink.

'That'll be a compliment, which would automatically catapult me to the top of the list in the Guinness Book of World Records for name-dropping,' replied Burnty and they all fell about laughing.

'Emily, I'm going now and I wish you a safe journey to Sydney,' said Robert as he walked downstairs. Robert had woken up early and was ready within a few hours. Emily came down to hug him and say goodbye.

'I wish you a safe journey too. We hope to see you soon. I'll be leaving later,' said Emily.

Burnty went to open the door while Robert rolled his heavy suitcase out of the house. Within a few minutes, they set off, reminiscing about the party at the Jomansa Hotel.

'Azuchukwu should be in Nigeria by now. He was due to fly back yesterday morning by a direct flight from Gatwick,' said Robert.

'Yes, that's true. I spoke to him when he arrived in London. I'll call him when I return home today. It was so nice of him to have come. You never know who's your true friend until you are in a crisis situation,' said Burnty.

'That's quite true. That's why they say "a friend in need is a friend indeed."'

They were on Waterloo Way, approaching the intersection with the London Road when Robert suddenly saw the New Walk Museum & Art Gallery. He said, 'I didn't manage to visit that Art Gallery.'

'Do you mean the New Walk Museum?'

'Yes. I think that's the name.'

'Maybe you can visit it when next you come back to the UK, if I haven't got a specialist registrar post in another town by then.'

Soon afterwards they arrived at the train station, where Burnty dragged out Robert's luggage and they both walked towards the ticket office. Robert bought a one-way ticket to Birmingham and as his train was not due for thirty minutes they went into the café for coffee and a final chat. An announcement warning passengers of the impending arrival of the Birmingham-bound train brought their conversation to an end. Robert dragged his suitcase to the platform with Burnty by his side. Within minutes the train had arrived.

Robert hugged and shook hands with Burnty, who helped him to push his heavy luggage onto the train. A few minutes later the train left and they both waved frantically until they disappeared from each other's view. Burnty felt emotional as he went back to his car and drove home alone. He was beginning to imagine what it would be like after Emily left later in the day. He mentally thanked the inventors of cell phone technology, who had made it possible to talk to anyone, anytime, anywhere in the world. Soon he'd be relying on this to cope with the departure of his better half.

On arriving home, he went to join Emily in the bedroom and helped her to pack her things in preparation for her journey.

Emily arrived at Manchester Airport and checked in at the British Airways desk for the Sydney-bound flight which was due later in the evening. Her train journey from Leicester had been smooth. Burnty had driven her to the station and their parting had been emotionally wrenching for both of them. Emily had actually broken down in tears, while Burnty tried hard to hold his back as they embraced for the last time. An elderly couple who witnessed the scene had been so moved that they gave Emily some tissues to wipe her eyes when she got onto the train. Now that she had checked in her luggage, all she had with her was a dark brown handbag. She walked towards the departure area where she underwent the routine security checks before going into one of the shops to buy perfume for her stepmother and father. She picked up a Gucci and a Bvlgari perfume and a copy of the latest *Vogue* magazine, then went to pay at the counter. The queue was quite long, but since her flight was still many hours ahead, she wasn't worried.

Suddenly out of nowhere, five naked men rushed into the store and demanded that the shop should be closed because they were protesting against the use of any chemical agent on the body, be it perfume or any form of cosmetics. They claimed to belong to an organization that felt that the human body should be left the way it was created and that it should not be interfered with by any beautifying agent. Many of the customers ran out of the stores when these burly men appeared. Each had a rectangular placard pasted on his chest with writing that was barely legible. They remained in the store while terrified customers gathered outside. One of the cashiers waited in the shop while the security men were called in. The five protesters were hastily led away by the security men.

Meanwhile, Emily had already dropped her shopping basket and fled the scene. She had read and heard about streakers, but she had never actually seen any before. She returned later when she saw that the crowd had dispersed. She found her shopping basket with the contents still inside and walked to the counter and paid for them. People began to discuss how the men had managed to get into the area in the first place. It was later discovered that they were passengers travelling from Manchester to Newcastle, where they planned to join other members of their organization in staging a huge naked protest in South Shields. Emily later went to one of the restaurants for a light meal before going to sit in the waiting area close to her departure gate. As she sat there she scanned her magazine then got out two novels, one by Barbara Cartland and the other by Danielle Steel. She had started both of them and was undecided about which one to read, so she decided to toss a coin, and after doing that she picked up the Barbara Cartland novel and began to read it. She had decided only to phone her father when she arrived in Sydney and had checked into her hotel. She had a confirmed booking at the Millennium Hotel, where she planned to stay for at least the first twenty-four hours. She was really looking forward to her trip and to working at the

Sydney Children's Hospital. After a few hours the electronic display indicated that passengers could begin to board the aircraft and Emily promptly joined the queue that had formed.

11

December 2003

Anonsa and Baguda were sitting in a black cab with their luggage squeezed into the available space. They were excited to be finally on their way to board a plane to their holiday destination. It had been difficult booking a hotel in Dublin due to an International Dance Festival which was taking place at the same time as their holiday. They had eventually managed to book a room at an hotel on St Stephen's Green.

'It's so nice to be leaving Dundee for a few days,' said Anonsa.

'It's a badly needed break. We've both been stressed in our jobs and I think we wholeheartedly deserve this holiday,' said Baguda as he planted a kiss on her lips.

'I remember you said that Dawn was also in Ireland with her boyfriend.'

'That's right. They are in Galway just now. Her boyfriend, Quentin, is a film director from Harrogate and they are planning to get married when Dawn finishes her studies later in the year.'

'That's interesting.'

'My parents and Quentin's parents can't wait to see it happen. Quentin's elder brother is already married to a woman of mixed race from Stevenage, so naturally his parents are greatly looking forward to having another mixed-race daughter-in-law.'

'It's always good to know that you are marrying into a family that unconditionally accepts you. I think your sister, Dawn, is lucky to have that.'

'It's just the way these things happen. It goes the other way sometimes. I remember my other sister had to break off her engagement because her boyfriend's parents were persistently nasty to her, no matter how much she tried to impress them.'

'We're approaching the departure terminal now,' said the taxi driver as he stopped at a red light. A few moments later he had pulled up in front of the terminal. After they paid, he helped them to unload their luggage and wished them a safe journey before driving off.

Baguda got a trolley and they loaded their luggage onto it, then wheeled it to the check-in counter. They checked in at the Ryan air desk, and were handed their boarding passes. Anonsa and Baguda made their way into the security check area where their boarding passes were examined and they underwent the necessary screening, before they went to locate their departure gate.

'It looks sunny outside. I hope it's warm too,' said Anonsa giggling as their plane touched down at Dublin International Airport.

'We'll soon find out,' replied Baguda. As the plane taxied on the runway, Anonsa heaved a sigh of contentment and glanced at Baguda who gave her a wink and gently squeezed her hand. As the plane came to a final stop, the passengers got up and began to remove their belongings from the overhead lockers.

Baguda, who was sitting in the aisle seat, helped Anonsa to reach her handbag, while passengers gradually made their way in a single file out of the aircraft. The passengers were driven away by a waiting bus to the luggage collection area where Baguda and Anonsa waited patiently for their luggage to arrive. At first the conveyor belt went round without any luggage on it, then the passengers' luggage began to roll by. They had to wait for nearly thirty minutes before the first of their cases arrived but within minutes the second case had arrived too. Baguda promptly wheeled their trolley out to the taxi rank, where they got a taxi to the hotel. The check-in at the hotel was swift and they were soon unpacking their bags in a spacious double bedded room. They undressed and slipped into the bathtub before getting changed into some clean clothes. They went downstairs to the hotel bar to have a drink.

'I hope you are well settled now,' said one of the porters who had helped them with their luggage earlier on.

'Yes, thank you,' said Baguda smiling.

'This place has a very friendly atmosphere, which is exactly what we need,' said Anonsa as she held Baguda's hand.

'Absolutely! We didn't come all this way with the stress of work wrapped tightly in our shoulder muscles to be showered with unneeded hostility, otherwise there would be no point coming on holiday.'

They sat in the bar and sipped their drinks.

'Look at that painting,' said Anonsa excitedly, as she pointed at one of the paintings hanging on the wall. 'Doesn't it look lovely?'

'It does. You and your paintings again! We'll have enough time for that later. I hope the National Gallery of Ireland is not too far from here.'

'No, it's not. It's on Merrion Square,' offered the bartender.

'Maybe we can even stroll there tonight,' quipped Anonsa.

'Why not just relax today and go there tomorrow?' said Baguda.

'That's a good idea. I understand they've got paintings by many great artists,' said Anonsa.

'You're quite right. They've got paintings by Rembrandt, El Greco, Reynolds and Goya,' said the bartender.

'You seem to be very knowledgeable about art,' said Baguda, who looked impressed.

'I've been to the National Gallery many times. I used to work in the café in the National History Museum which is not too far from there, so whenever I had a break from work, I used to go there and feast my eyes on the paintings. I'm a bit of an amateur artist myself and I'll be starting a degree course in Art at Trinity College this autumn.'

'That's impressive. Maybe we'll be coming to your exhibitions in the future when you're a big name in the Art world,' said Anonsa.

'Thank you. If only I were so talented,' said the bartender modestly.

After they finished their drinks, they went out and strolled hand-in-hand to St Stephen's Green. They stayed there until it was dark and then made their way back to the hotel. On reaching their room they switched on the TV which was tuned to one of the local channels that was showing a programme in Gaelic. They switched to another station which was reviewing a movie about the Irish Potato Famine of the nineteenth century, which was showing in cinemas all over Ireland. They eventually went to bed and slept soundly until the following morning when they woke up and planned their day out. First they went to the National Gallery and looked at paintings by Reynolds, Goya, Rembrandt,

Gainsborough, Hogarth, Holbein and Picasso. El Greco's paint-ings and other artists' works were kept in a different area, and they promised themselves that they'd visit again before returning to the UK. Baguda really enjoyed their visit to the gallery. He had always thought that he didn't much care about works of art, so he was surprised how much he had enjoyed looking at the paintings. They also went to the Heraldic Museum and the Mansion House before going to lunch at Dillon's Restaurant on Suffolk Street. On their way back to the hotel, they passed through the St Stephen's Green Shopping Centre and bought a few items as souvenirs. On reaching the hotel, Anonsa went into the bar to compare the painting she had seen the day before with the ones she had seen at the National Gallery that morning. Baguda couldn't stop himself from laughing as he accompanied her there, while Anonsa giggled like a young girl on her first day at school.

'I didn't know that your interest in art was so strong,' said Baguda, still smiling.

'That's an understatement. If I were to use bombastic language, I'd say it's gargantuan and mammothly inspiring.'

'Hm! Madam Shakespeare sounding grandiloquent again. I wish I had a dictionary with me.'

'I'll get you one when we go upstairs.'

As soon as they reached their room Baguda went into the bathroom and came out with the fly of his trousers undone. As he approached the bed Anonsa looked up and gazed at his erect penis which protruded from his trousers like a piece of iron pole.

'This is the dic-tion-ary. I already have one,' said Baguda laughing.

He rubbed his genitals on Anonsa's lips and they began to

have sex. They both groaned with pleasure as they made love over and over again.

Baguda and Anonsa woke up the following morning to the sound of birds chirping in the nearby park. They felt wonderfully refreshed. Baguda grabbed the TV remote control and they watched the news and the weather forecast while they lay in bed. Anonsa then got out of bed and peered through the window at the sky as if she was trying to decipher the secrets of what the day had in store for them. As she stood there, Baguda came from behind and caressed her full naked breasts, then she turned round to face him and they kissed each other passionately. They both rolled into bed again, laughing and fondling each other with desire. Eventually they got out of bed and got showered and dressed ready for the day's outing. They ate breakfast which was brought to the room by a hotel steward, then walked to the lift which took them downstairs. As they came out of the lift they met a middle-aged, black couple who were speaking what sounded to Baguda like Swahili, a language widely spoken in East and Southern Africa. They were both wearing African costume.

'It sounded to me as if that couple were speaking Swahili,' said Baguda, as they stepped out of the hotel.

'Really?'

'I think so. It definitely wasn't Zulu or Xhosa.'

'I can see that you are quite conversant with Southern African languages.'

'I used to accompany my dad on business trips to Southern Africa. That was how I became familiar with the languages. I don't actually speak them but I can recognize them whenever I hear them being spoken.'

'There are over two hundred languages in Nigeria but I can only speak three of them.'

'And which ones are those?'

'They are Yoruba, which of course is the language spoken where I come from, Hausa and Ebira.'

'How about Efik?'

'No, I don't speak it. But you should be able to. I know that your mum's parents are Efik.'

'That's right. But, unfortunately, I cannot speak the language. Even my mum does not speak it fluently. I guess it's probably because she was born and brought up in the UK. But my dad who's a white European speaks Swahili very fluently. It just goes to show that knowledge of languages is not necessarily about colour of skin or origin, it is about having contact with the language and learning it.'

'I quite agree with you. For instance, I understand Ebira because many of my friends were from Okene. I never lived in that part of Nigeria, yet I could speak the language.'

'Where's Okene?'

'It's a small town that became part of Kogi State, which was created in 1991. It used to be part of Kwara State, where I come from. It's a hilly region with huge deposits of iron ore.'

'That's interesting. It's a shame that I've never been to Nigeria, but Dawn has been.'

'How come?'

'She just made the decision to go and she told me that she was showered with affection in Calabar by my mum's relatives. I'm itching to receive that avalanche of familial affection someday when I eventually visit Nigeria. Luckily, both of my maternal grandparents are still alive. They were always so kind and affectionate whenever they came to visit us in the UK and I liked to dote on them too, but I want to visit them in Calabar very soon.'

'You are lucky to have caring grandparents still living.'

'Nothing compares to the tender and warm affection of grand-parents and being able to reciprocate in kind when they are very old fills one with enormous joy and satisfaction.'

Baguda and Anonsa were coming out of Dublin Castle. They walked towards Patrick Street, where they caught a bus to Trinity College. They toured the campus, and Baguda showed Anonsa where he had been when he came on an excursion to Dublin as an undergraduate. He also planned to call in at the office of his father's friend, who was a solicitor in Dublin, if he could find it. He remembered that it was not too far from the River Liffey. After their visit to Trinity College, they headed to Dublin Zoo, in Phoenix Park. They spent the rest of the day there and arrived back at the hotel quite late. They were so tired that they collapsed in bed without removing their clothes and fell asleep right away. They slept so deeply that their alarm clock didn't wake them and they eventually woke up late in the afternoon of the following day. After they had showered and dressed, they watched a programme on TV then went out to dine at a restaurant in Donnybrook which specialized in fish, steaks, vegetarian and gluten-free dishes. Baguda had dined there in the past and he knew the food was excellent, so naturally he recommended it to Anonsa. They both had a meal of fish and salad. Anonsa thoroughly enjoyed it and was particularly impressed by the impec-cable manners of the waitresses.

On leaving the restaurant, Baguda promised to take them to an Italian restaurant that he had also visited in the past some other day. They also planned to go to the cinema later in the week to see the movie about the Irish Potato Famine. But for now they decided to catch a bus back to the hotel. The first bus that arrived was packed with a group of unruly youths who were screaming obscenities at the other passengers. They waited for a second bus which was relatively empty. The driver was a portly man in his mid-forties with ginger hair, who flashed a tobacco-stained set of teeth at the passengers as they got on. He spoke genially in a very thick Irish accent.

'The driver is very friendly,' said Anonsa as she sat down, clutching her handbag tightly as if to prevent it from being wrenched away from her by marauding vagabonds.

'It appears so,' said Baguda, sounding indifferent. 'I know that you are quite sensitive to the way others behave, which is perfectly understandable when you've been surrounded by affection all your life. Your threshold for tolerating insensitive and hostile behaviour is very low indeed.'

Anonsa burst into a suppressed laughter.

'How about you? Do you enjoy being treated in a hostile and unfriendly manner?'

'Definitely not.'

'Which means it's human nature to want to be treated nicely and affectionately. But before you can expect to be treated nicely you should treat others nicely first. This is a simple law of nature, that's been known to be true in all ages.'

'You are quite right,' said Baguda, as he planted a kiss on her lips.

'We are both oozing with philosophical and intellectual energies.'

'That reminds me of physics lessons. Is ours kinetic or potential energy? Oh, sorry, I forgot that you are not a scientist, so I won't bore you with esoteric and mundane scientific issues on a fun-filled day.'

'Never mind. Though it might interest you to know that I actually studied physics during my third year in High School, before dropping it.'

'I can't believe it,' said Anonsa, looking astonished.

'Alright, I'll regale you with Newton's second law of motion so that you can believe it.'

'Please go ahead.'

'Listen while I drop it red hot on your tympanic membrane . . .'

'So now you're an ENT surgeon as well as a physicist?' cut in Anonsa smiling.

'Listen. It states that: *"the rate of change of momentum of a body is directly proportional to the applied force and it takes place in the direction in which the force acts."'*

'This is quite remarkable,' exclaimed Anonsa, looking stunned. 'Need I say again that your versatility and breadth of knowledge is quite unique? I wholeheartedly admire your stupendously retentive memory.'

'Thank you for the compliment. Need I say too that I admire your linguistic elegance? I think you should be a lawyer,' complimented Baguda.

'Thank you too.' They were now in front of the hotel. As they entered the lift on their way to their room, they met one of the hotel maids inside. She smiled at them as they got out of the lift.

'Today is our last day in Dublin!' said Anonsa, as she and Baguda crossed the road to the bus station on Amiens Street.

'Let's review all the places we've been to so far,' said Baguda.

'There are so many that I can't remember them all.'

'But you can remember Le Caprice Restaurant.'

'Of course! That was the place where the waiter slipped and

fell carrying a tray full of hot food and champagne. It's not easy to forget all the shattered glass and debris we had to avoid on our way out of the restaurant.'

'But the meal was very good.'

'Definitely. I'm not complaining at all.'

They were now in the bus station waiting to catch a bus into the nearby countryside. The bus arrived in good time and they bought their tickets from the driver and sat down. Anonsa sat at the window side looking out.

'Let's see what the day has in store for us,' said Baguda.

'Ireland has very picturesque countryside. This trip has really succeeded in melting away all the stress embedded in my shoulder muscles. When I go back to work my stress load will virtually weigh in at zero,' said Anonsa smiling.

'Mine will be very low but not quite zero, as one of my partners is going on holiday soon, so I'll have a lot of extra work on.'

'At least you've burst some of your stress balloons by coming here to Dublin.'

'There's just no doubt about that.'

Anonsa and Baguda spent the better part of the day travelling round the countryside near Dublin. They returned much later in the day and went straight back to their hotel. They then rested for a few hours after which they showered and went to the hotel restaurant for the first time since their arrival.

'The hotel food is very good,' said Anonsa when they had begun to eat.

'I think so too,' said Baguda as he munched his food. When they had finished they went to Parnell Street to check out the cinema there, but it was not showing the movie they were interested in. They decided to try the Savoy, which was on Upper O'Connell Street.

'You weren't able to call on your father's friend,' said Anonsa as they crossed the road to catch a bus.

'Oh! Poor Mr O'Meara. He'll understand. I'll phone him before we leave Dublin tomorrow.'

On arriving at the Savoy they were able to get tickets to see *The Irish Potato Famine* which was showing in a few hours' time. It was getting dark as they strolled around holding hands. After a few hours people began to file into the cinema. Baguda and Anonsa took their allocated seats before the film started. It was a long film that lasted for about three and a half hours, but they both found it very moving. After the film was over, they took a taxi back to their hotel so they could start packing for the morning flight back to Dundee the following day.

They arrived at the hotel feeling exhausted, and Anonsa was so tired that she wondered how she'd manage to climb the stairs if the lift had broken down. She felt so lethargic that she virtually dragged her feet all the way to their room. When they finally arrived at their room the packing was done mostly by Baguda, as Anonsa was so tired she drifted off to sleep after collapsing in bed. As well as the cases they'd brought, they now had a third bag that contained all the gifts they had bought for their relatives and friends.

After Baguda had packed the major items, he stripped to his underpants and lay in bed beside Anonsa. As he watched Anonsa sleeping he became aroused and started caressing her. She opened her eyes and smiled. Baguda became so hot with passion that he wanted to have sex with her but Anonsa pleaded that she was tired. Baguda felt snubbed and upset so he decided to hurt Anonsa's feelings too and he went to sleep feeling horny. When Anonsa woke up the following morning, Baguda was not in the room. She called out his name but there was no response. She got up from the bed, opened the door and entered the corridor. Standing in front of her was Baguda kissing a girl whom Anonsa guessed by her dress, was probably one of the hotel maids. Anonsa froze in shock. When the girl saw her, she quickly pulled away from Baguda and disappeared into the lift. Baguda turned to face Anonsa.

'What's all this?' she screamed at him. 'In such a short time we've been here?'

'What do you think it is?' countered Baguda his eyes blood-shot.

Anonsa ran back into their room and broke down, weeping uncontrollably. She knew right away that their relationship was over. Knowing herself well, she knew that it was better for her to end the relationship, even though reluctantly. She felt a searing pain in her chest as if she was going to melt. She wondered how Baguda was able to win the girl's heart so quickly, since she and Baguda had been together most of the time since they arrived. Baguda watched her as she wept and began to feel guilty for hurting her feelings in such a crude way. He knew he could be very insensitive, egotistic and selfish, which he often regretted after the damage had been done.

He began to think of the good times they had had together over the past few days, only for everything to end in such a sad way because of his rigid and unfeeling demand for instant sexual gratification. After Anonsa stopped crying she became cold and silent. Her head was bowed in grief and she did not speak to Baguda again. They left the hotel trying to conceal the antipathy that had developed between them overnight. As they got into the taxi which took them to the airport, the silence between them had grown like an icy barrier that could not be broken.

They remained in this state of non-communication even after they had boarded the plane. On their arrival in Dundee, the atmosphere of silence remained until it was fleetingly broken by the taxi driver who took them home from the airport. When they got home, Anonsa went straight to the bedroom next to the one they had previously shared before they went on what had turned out to be their doomed holiday. She transferred all her belongings into her new bedroom and began to ponder over her next plan of action. Over the years she had overlooked some of Baguda's insensitive actions, but she was so completely taken aback by his recent display of sheer callous, insensitivity that she knew she would have to end the relationship for the sake of her own psychological and emotional well-being. After making up her mind she went to sleep.

Baguda, on the other hand, got into his car and drove to his favourite pub as he always did when he was feeling stressed. He had often wished that he were less callous and brutal in his actions. As he pondered over what Anonsa would do next, tears began to run down his cheeks. He knew how dedicated and caring Anonsa had been and he also knew that underneath his occasional ruthlessness he was deeply in love with her. He had even thought about the possibility of them getting married and having children. Now he did not know how to beg for forgiveness and he wasn't even sure whether she would forgive him considering the intensity of negative emotions he had elicited in her by his behaviour in Dublin. Baguda wiped his face and kept on driving hoping that Anonsa's hostility towards him would disappear in time.

12

Burnty was taking a bath. He had just arrived home from work and had decided to get washed and change into another set of clothes. It had been a little over three weeks since Emily travelled to Australia and it would be another five weeks before she returned to the UK. They had been speaking regularly to each other by phone since she arrived in Sydney and he had been surprised by how well he was managing to cope on his own. After drying himself with a freshly laundered white towel and putting on a pair of black jeans and a light blue T-shirt, Burnty went into the kitchen to prepare a meal for himself. After dinner he dialled his cousin, Dominic's cell phone number but it went through to voicemail. He left a message and went back into the sitting room and switched on the TV. He watched the news on CNN, then went upstairs to the bedroom to get his Parker pen which he had left on the bedside table. As he came downstairs, he heard his cell phone ringing. He rushed quickly to pick it up and saw Dominic's number on display.

'Hi Dominic, did you get my message?' said Burnty.

'Yes I got it and that's why I'm calling you back. You must have phoned while I was on the underground. I'm just back from Heathrow and I'm heading to the British Museum.'

'What were you doing at Heathrow?'

'I accompanied my boss, Drian Huskett, to the airport. He's travelling to Auckland in New Zealand for a week to attend a conference.'

'Who's going to stand in for him during his absence?'

'He made sure that he had his desk cleared of all outstanding work before he left. He also delegated some major tasks that couldn't wait until he comes back. So everything is under control.'

'What's happening at the British Museum?'

'There's an exhibition that's currently going on there and one of the organizers is my friend. He's got a project on sculpture that we are both working on.'

'Was he the one who trained in Ahmadu Bello University Art School?'

'No. That's Jinjiwa. He works at the Victoria and Albert Museum in Kensington.'

'That reminds me of the name I was going to suggest for your daughter, Ingrid.'

'What name is it?' inquired Dominic, laughing. 'I hope it's a good name?'

'I hope so too. It's to honour your wife Isabel.'

'So you want her to be called Isabel too?'

'No. I'm suggesting Albertina.'

'Why?'

'Your wife is inadvertently linked to two great Alberts in history, both of whom happen to be German-born. Isabel was born in Ulm in the same town as Albert Einstein, and she graduated from the University of Bonn, where Prince Albert, Queen Victoria's

143

husband, also graduated. I just felt that calling your daughter, Ingrid Albertina would be very appropriate.'

'What a sound and well thought out link. I think I'll buy your idea and I'm sure that Isabel will like it too. She's always very proud of her place of birth,' said Dominic. 'In fact the name you've proposed reminds me of when I went to the dermatology clinic at the Ahmadu Bello University Teaching Hospital in Zaria with my friend Jinjiwa, while we were both undergraduates. I remember that on our arrival in the hospital by the Tudun Wada gate, close to Zaria City, we met a group of young house officers who were chatting among themselves and one of them was called Albertina. I remember that prior to then I had never met anyone who bore that particular name.'

'That's interesting. What were you being treated for?'

'It wasn't me, it was my friend. He had a long-standing case of psoriasis and he had asked me to go with him to see his physician.'

'I read in one of the Nigerian dailies, last time I was there, that they've moved to their permanent site and that the one in Kaduna had been closed down.'

'That's interesting. I was completely unaware of that. Ever since I left Zaria as a graduate I've never gone back there and I only remembered this episode after you mentioned the name Albertina.'

'Have you spoken to Robert recently?'

'Yes. I phoned him last week and he was so happy. He told me that he passed his exam and he'll soon be an Attending Physician.'

'That was what I was going to tell you. I just wanted to know whether you already knew about it.'

'How about your own interviews for the specialist registrar post?'

'I'm quite optimistic. I've been put on the waiting list in two London hospitals, and I still have some more interviews to attend.'

'And where are those hospitals?'

'One is the Royal Free Hospital in Hampstead and the other one is the Whittington Hospital. If any of the people who were given the jobs don't turn up, then I'm next on the list.'

'I wish you success all the time.'

'Thank you. I think I really need all your good wishes.'

Dominic had arrived at the British Museum.

'I'm inside the museum now.'

'I can hear some noise in the background, let me leave you. I'll speak to you soon,' said Burnty before he switched off his phone.

After leaving the British Museum, Dominic travelled home to Bayswater stopping to buy some fruit and vegetables in one of the local shops on his way. As he walked home he thought about the name that Burnty had suggested for his daughter Ingrid. He was eager to reach home and tell Isabel about it.

13

October 2003

'It's great to be back in the UK again,' said Emily, looking delighted as the train approached Leicester.

She and Burnty had been travelling together from Manchester Airport, where he had gone to meet her. Her trip from Sydney had been uneventful except for a slight delay after the aircraft had touched down. After disembarking from the plane, she didn't have to wait long at the baggage reclaim area and on reaching the arrival terminal she had met Burnty who was waiting for her. They had hugged and kissed each other.

On arriving in Sydney she had only stayed in a hotel for one night before she moved into the accommodation provided by the hospital.

So she hadn't ended up staying with her father and stepmother at all, though she had visited them very frequently.

The train arrived in Leicester, which was its final destination.

'It's so good to be able to experience clinical medical practice in another environment. My experience in Sydney was very enriching,' said Emily, as Burnty helped to lift her luggage out of the train.

'It's good to know that you enjoyed your time in Sydney. Of course you've already told me almost everything that happened there. I'm also glad to know that you've been able to make it up with your dad.'

Emily went momentarily cold as Burnty finished speaking. She was happy that he was unaware of how hostile her father was to their relationship. Her father had succeeded in hiding his feelings in the past, on the few occasions that he had phoned their house and spoken to Burnty, when Emily was not at home.

'Are you alright?' asked Burnty as Emily became silent.

'I'm fine,' said Emily quickly, trying to mask her momentary feeling of uneasiness.

They got into a waiting taxi which drove them home.

'Did you visit Sydney University?'

'I only went there once. It's an old university, founded in 1850.'

'That's interesting. Do you know Mr McNabe, the consultant paediatric surgeon?'

'Is he the big, tall man who walks with a swagger?'

'Yes, that's him. He graduated from Sydney University.'

'That's interesting.'

'I was going to ask you about all the places you'd been to but I suddenly realized that you've told me about nearly all of them.'

'I didn't really have much time to visit places. I was very busy in the hospital and by the time I got to know my way around the hospital, it was time to come back to the UK. Some of the friends I made there took me to the Valhalla Cinema and Bondi Beach. We also visited some cafés. I particularly remember one called the GoGo Café on Oxford Street, where we met a group of medical students from Leeds University. They told me that they went there because of the name of the street which reminded them of Oxford Street in London.'

'That's interesting. It's remarkable that in spite of your busy schedule you still found time to visit a few places.'

'The workload turned out to be heavier than I had expected, though I really enjoyed my work there. I couldn't even spend as much time as I wanted to with my dad and his family. But we spoke to each other nearly every day.'

'That's nice.'

'And I really loved it.'

When they arrived home and Emily entered the house, she heaved a big sigh and went straight for her mail which Burnty had neatly arranged in a pile. Most of her correspondence was from the Philatelic Club. One was from the club's Secretary-General who wanted the members of the Executive Committee to meet soon, provided that it was convenient for Emily. He knew when Emily was arriving back in the UK, so he had chosen an appropriate date for the meeting. Emily decided to phone him later on to tell him that the date suited her fine. She was secretly delighted by the opportunity it would afford her to see Richard again. She had been speaking to Richard on a very regular basis throughout the period of her stay in Australia and their love affair had progressed much further. This state of affairs was encouraged by her father's immense hostility to her relationship with Burnty. She loved Burnty very much but she had been so happy about her reunion with her father, that she was prepared to do anything in her power to keep it that way. She loved Richard too, as she had found out over the last eight weeks and she knew that her father would not disapprove of her relationship with him, if he eventually found out.

She had hoped that her father would realize that if he could live in a foreign country and find happiness, contentment and a wife there, then he would be more tolerant of non-natives who had made the UK their home, and realize that they too have the right to find love and happiness where they live. However, to her deep disappointment she dared not confront her father with his prejudice which he had never acknowledged; he saw himself as being a very liberal and tolerant person.

Another letter informed her about the arrival of some books that she had requested from the hospital library.

'You don't look tired at all,' said Burnty.

'I slept on the plane,' said Emily.

After reading her letters, Emily had a shower, got dressed and went down to the sitting room. She later joined Burnty in the kitchen where he was making cups of tea for both of them. They sat together on the sofa in the sitting room and watched a TV programme about a children's hospital in Niamey in Niger.

'Did you know that people often confuse Niger with Nigeria? Maybe it's because they are neighbours. Niger is French speaking while Nigeria is English speaking,' said Burnty. Emily suddenly raised her head as if she was trying to remember something.

'I'm trying to recollect where I met someone from Niger.'

'Have you met someone from that country?'

'Yes. Oh, I remember now,' exclaimed Emily and her face lit up. 'I met a lady in Sydney from Niger. She had brought her grandson to the hospital for treatment for a minor complaint. She was very friendly and pleasant. Her husband was a diplomat in Canberra and they were visiting a family friend in Sydney when their grandson felt a bit unwell. Even though the boy looked perfectly healthy, they still thought that they should bring him to the hospital, which showed how caring they were.'

'That's interesting. The world is a global village as you can see.'

'Her husband was so proud to tell me that one of his children was a doctor too. He said he had three children, by his wife, all of whom were university graduates and his other children by other women were also doing well academically.'

'They must be a highly motivated couple to be able to achieve that in a country like Niger.'

'I guess that's why he was so proud of their children's achievements. He was denied the opportunity of going to university even though he was quite clever because of the early death of his own father when he was still very young. He had risen through the ranks in his place of work.'

'You are a thoroughly humane physician. It's amazing that you had time during your consultation to listen to all of this' complimented Burnty.

'Well, I believe that a doctor is someone who elucidates human problems. As you well know, physical illnesses can have underlying emotional and psychological causes, so it's a good thing to be able to listen. That's all I did, I just listened to them,' said Emily trying to sound modest.

'It's nice to have you back. How was your trip to Sydney?' asked Craig Croft, the Secretary-General of the Philatelic Club as Emily arrived at the Town Hall for the Executive Committee meeting.

'Thank you. It was really interesting and I had a very pleasant time. But I'm happy to be back with you all again,' said Emily, as she took her seat.

Richard had arrived early but he hadn't been in the room when Emily arrived.

'Welcome back! It's marvellous to have you back. We really missed you,' Richard exclaimed as he came into the room.

'Thank you. It's really nice to be back,' said Emily as she got up and hugged him.

After a while, the other officers of the club arrived. No one was absent on this occasion. Unlike the last executive committee meeting when the social secretary was absent.

'It's great that everyone is here today for this meeting,' said Emily.

'We haven't had one hundred per cent attendance since this committee took office. It's amazing and I do hope it continues,' said the Secretary-General, who had been on all the Executive Committees for the past three years. Everyone looked happy and relaxed as the meeting began. Emily's leadership skills were highly admired by the other members of the club. They found her approachable, unassuming, understanding, assertive when necessary, firm but also sensitive to and respectful of the opinions of the other members even if she did not agree with them.

They discussed many things, including some new programmes that the club had embarked upon. A wealthy industrialist in the city had promised to donate a property to be used as a permanent Secretariat for the club and this was extensively discussed. The club Ramble was due to take place the following weekend and Emily's one-week residence at Churchill College, Cambridge was still many weeks away.

When the meeting drew to a close, everyone was glad that so many issues had been thrashed out. This would make the proceedings at the next General Meeting much easier. They all shook hands before leaving the hall. Emily and Richard walked out side by side. It was getting dark and as they stood by Richard's car, they almost disappeared into the darkness. They began to kiss and touch each other hungrily. After a while they got into their respective cars and drove to a more secluded spot where no one would see them.

Emily then got into Richard's car, which had its back seat down to make room for both of them. As they slipped into the car filled with lustful thoughts, Emily undid Richard's fly while he caressed her breasts. His stone-hard penis jutted out and into Emily's mouth and she sucked at it. As he came into her mouth he gave a groan of pleasure. He then proceeded to enter her and they made love like two wild animals.

When they were both spent, their faces radiated satisfaction and contentment. Emily began to examine her clothes for semen stains and she was relieved to find that it was only her under-wear that was stained. They quickly got dressed and kissed each other, before Emily got back into her car and they drove away in different directions.

As Emily drove home, she was racked by feelings of guilt which combined uneasily with sensations of delight. She began to wonder whether her relationship with Burnty could continue, considering the very hostile attitude of her father towards it. Having enjoyed a wonderful father-daughter relationship in Sydney during the past few weeks, she did not want anything to lead to her estrange-ment from him again. Since she now had someone in her life who deeply loved and cared about her as much as Burnty did, and whom she knew would be approved of by her father, she began to think of the inevitable: she would have to leave Burnty and move in with Richard. As she thought about this difficult option, she suddenly felt a sense of emotional freedom flow through her body. If she moved in with Richard, she would be able to bring the affair into the open and then she would be able to plan her future with her entire family behind her, including her father. She felt that as liberating as this option might sound emotion-ally, she would have to pay a huge price in terms of guilt. She knew in her heart that if her father had not been hostile to her relationship with Burnty, she would have been prepared to marry him and settle down. Yet, she felt that if she was to free herself from her present self-inflicted emotional bondage, she would have to take the plunge and end her relationship with Burnty.

Richard had showered her with gifts while she was in Sydney as he hadn't been able to do that while she was in the UK. He was completely smitten with her and bowled over by her wonderful personality. To demonstrate how desperate he was for Emily to move in with him, he had split up with his girlfriend. So now he was single again and completely free; waiting for the loving arms of Emily.

As Emily searched for reasons to justify her impending action she began to think of Cecilia Ovora, one of Burnty's former class-mates at the University of Lagos, who had attended their party. Cecilia was a dentist who lived with her husband and two children in Blackpool. She had never visited Leicester prior to the party and neither was she in regular communication with Burnty. Emily knew that the suspicion of an affair between her and Burnty would be tenuous and far fetched, but she needed something to relieve her guilty conscience. Just before arriving home she saw a billboard that read: '*FAIRNESS IS WHAT WE ALL WANT. BUT CAN WE GIVE IT?*' The statement struck her like a thunderbolt. This was hardly the kind of moralizing statement she needed as she tried to grapple with a difficult issue in her life: her impending split from Burnty! When Emily arrived home she was met by a most unpleasant surprise. She had not expected Burnty back from the hospital until the following day and nearly fainted with shock when she saw him coming downstairs. He had rushed home to pick up a book and was on his way back to the hospital again.

'Hi honey, how was the meeting?' asked Burnty.

'What are you doing at home? I thought you were supposed to be at the hospital?' said Emily, sounding unfriendly. She frowned.

Burnty was taken aback. He had never seen her look and act so coldly since they had been together. She seemed to speak with repressed hostility.

'Are you alright honey?' inquired Burnty, looking concerned.

'Of course I am,' snapped Emily, avoiding eye contact with Burnty as she moved into the sitting room.

'I'll see you tomorrow then. I'm off to the hospital,' said Burnty, as he opened the door and left the house. As he drove off, Emily peered out of the window and watched his car disappear into the darkness. She sat on the sofa and broke down in tears. After crying profusely she went to the bathroom, removed her clothes and put them into the washing machine along with some other dirty laundry.

Even though she had nearly betrayed herself by her near-emotional and psychological collapse on meeting Burnty at home unexpectedly, she still believed that he was unaware of what had happened between her and Richard a few hours earlier. She made herself some tea and toast and switched on the TV to try and distract herself.

It was about a month since Emily had moved out of the house to go and live with Richard. Burnty had woken up one morning to find a very formal note which had been left by Emily before she drove to work at the hospital. Burnty had been off duty and had slept into the late hours of the morning, so he woke up long after Emily had left for work. In the neatly hand-written note Emily had informed him that she would be moving out of the house to join the new man in her life, that their relationship could not continue and that he should not bother looking for her. Burnty had been thunderstruck and completely shattered by the unexpected note. At first he thought that he was in a dream. He had re-read the note several times but the stark message still stared him in the face and he simply felt numb. The relationship that he had nurtured for years had suddenly collapsed. He found it difficult to believe and even comprehend. They had had a row one day, it was shortly after the evening on which Emily had sex with Richard, but Burnty knew nothing about that. Burnty had racked his brain looking for clues as to what might have led to Emily's decision. He had found none, except for her bizarre aggression on the evening when she went to her club meeting in the Town Hall. At the same time as Emily moved out of the house she was starting a new job at the Glenfield Hospital, three miles northwest of the city centre. This made it impossible for him to see her and try to resolve any issues between them.

Burnty remembered vividly what had happened on the awful day when Emily left. He had rung her cell phone after reading the note but her phone was switched off. He hadn't been able to go back to sleep so had travelled to London to tell Dominic what had happened. Dominic and Isabel had been very supportive. They were really shocked by the turn of events. They had lavished him with empathy and had advised him to take a holiday, either to the USA to see his younger brother, Robert, or to Nigeria to see his parents and other members of his family. He had spent a few days with them and they looked after him very well before he returned to Leicester.

He was eventually able to speak to Emily, though initially she had refused to respond to his phone calls. She told him in clear and uncompromising terms that their love affair was over but that they could still remain friends. She also made it clear that her decision was irrevocable and since then she had taken all her personal belongings from the house. Burnty still lived in the house but since they had a joint mortgage on it, Emily said that they would reach a monetary agreement about the house in the near future. Burnty was in the sitting room, calmly watching TV. He had already made up his mind about what he wanted to do. He had decided to travel to the USA to see his brother and also to Nigeria to see the rest of his family. He hoped fervently that providence would smile on him and that he would find a new love in his life. He had come to accept the situation. He thought about his job interviews. He had not been successful so far except for the two London hospitals where his name had been put on the waiting list. Being an optimist, he continued to hope for the best.

Burnty went into the kitchen and made a cup of tea for himself, chose a poetry book from the study, which he started to read. Since Emily had left him he had become more involved in some of his hobbies. He had begun playing football at the local club run by the Royal Infirmary. Being an amateur artist, he had made attempts at painting too with some help and encouragement from Dominic. He had also been recollecting everything his parents had taught him while he was growing up about the fluidity and uncertainty of human behaviour. Even though he had completely trusted Emily, and had been crushed by the blow of her sudden, unexpected departure, he was far from suffering a nervous breakdown. As he read through the poetry book he contemplated his future.

14

'Good afternoon ladies and gentlemen, Flight 353 from Chicago O'Hare Airport, which was scheduled to arrive by 1540 hours, has been delayed. Further announcements will be made in due course,' came a clinically delivered announcement at Cardiff Airport.

Anonsa had arrived early at the airport to meet her mother who was due to arrive on the flight that had been delayed. On hearing the announcement, she began to pace up and down.

'I wonder why it's delayed? I'm dying to see mummy. It's quite some time now since we last saw each other,' Anonsa muttered to herself.

Her mother, Susan, had been to New York to see her sons, Peter and Richmond, Anonsa's twin brothers, who were both living in the USA. Peter, who lived in North Carolina had joined his brother in New York to be there for her visit. She had spent about three weeks in America, visiting relatives and friends. Her final stop was in Chicago, where she had gone to see her first cousin. They hadn't seen each other since they left Harvard

University together and Susan had to go back to Nigeria to join her husband. Since she rarely travelled anywhere apart from the UK, she had tried to visit as many relatives and friends as possible.

After a while Anonsa walked into the nearby Starbucks café and ordered a cup of coffee to calm her nerves, as she always did whenever she was anxious about anything.

Anonsa paid for her coffee and left the café.

'Anonsa! Anonsa!!' called out a tall, slim, blonde.

Anonsa looked around trying to see who was calling her name. Then, as she turned round she saw Theresa, a colleague during her senior house officer days at a hospital in Scotland.

Anonsa was visibly excited as she walked briskly to meet her friend and they both hugged each other tightly. 'Hi Theresa, it's so nice to see you,' Anonsa said.

'It's great to see you too,' said Theresa. 'What have you been up to, and what are you doing here?'

'I work as a specialist registrar in obstetrics and gynaecology in a hospital in Aberystwyth. I'm married now and have a young daughter. I've been seeing my sister-in-law onto her plane back to Zurich, she's been staying with us for a few weeks.'

Anonsa and Theresa walked towards the adjacent seating area and sat down together to continue talking.

'I'm so happy to see you after such a long time. I'm here to meet my mum but her flight has been delayed. Do you remember other colleagues of ours from those days, especially Mathias?'

'Oh yes, Mathias! I do remember him, he came a few weeks late after the change over between the new and the old senior house officers. I heard that he's now a specialist registrar in cardiology in one of the hospitals in Leeds. I remember he had a big crush on you at the time.'

'Oh, come on,' Anonsa chuckled to herself.

'Ladies and gentlemen, flight 353 from Chicago O'Hare Airport will now be arriving at 1845 hours,' came the same clinical voice.

'Oh, what a relief,' sighed Anonsa, who was delighted by the news.

'Let's swap mobile phone numbers,' suggested Theresa.

'What about your home number?' asked Anonsa.

'We're hoping to move, so it may change soon, but for now it's . . .' said Theresa writing the number on one of the pages of Anonsa's diary.

'That's fine.'

'I must be going now. I'll definitely give you a call and I wish you the best in your career.'

'Thank you so much. It's always a breath of fresh air to see you. I wish you and your family the very best. I'll look forward to speaking to you again.'

They hugged each other and walked together to the taxi rank where Theresa got into a black cab, waving frantically as it was driven off. Anonsa was exhilarated by the encounter with her old friend. They worked together as senior house officers at Ninewells Hospital in Dundee and became very good friends even though Theresa worked in a different department.

Theresa was from Aberdeen but had graduated from the University of Dundee. Her parents always came to visit her while she was in Dundee and Anonsa was quite close to them. Theresa's father, Patrick, had lived in Nigeria briefly during his undergraduate days at Cambridge when he worked as a volunteer for Stop the War Foundation, a charity organization which assisted displaced people during the Biafran civil war in Nigeria in the late 1960s.

Her mother, Wendy, had spent a year on an exchange

programme in Kaduna in Nigeria, while she was still at school in London. Theresa's father was Scottish and her mother was English and both were now retired. Anonsa remembered an incident that particularly brought herself and Theresa so close to each other. It was a Saturday evening and Anonsa was on-call on her first day at work, when a patient suddenly went into a cardiac arrest and Anonsa had to be called in. Theresa, who had been off duty after some nights of being on-call, just strolled into the ward where everyone was running helter-skelter to assist the resuscitation team. That was when she met Anonsa for the first time.

The two women took to each other straightaway and from then on they became especially close and even went on a few holidays together in the UK. Anonsa remembered how she had encountered Mathias earlier that same day. She had arrived on the ward early in the morning to take over from the doctor who had been on duty the night before, and Mathias suddenly appeared from the ward and said, 'Hello, I'm Mathias. Are you the new doctor?'

'Yes, I am. Are you Dr Pierson?'

'No. I swapped with him. I know his name is still on the rota. He'll be doing my on-calls next weekend.'

'Oh! I see. Anyhow, I'm pleased to meet you.'

Mathias then began to hand over the patients to her before he went home. She remembered Mathias staring fixedly at her and being completely suffused with delight at meeting her. Anonsa was not unfamiliar with such open admiration from the men she worked with. Mathias never plucked up the courage to ask her out, but everyone knew that he was interested in her and he himself admitted that he had a crush on her. Despite this, they did enjoy a good working relationship.

Anonsa remembered all this as she sat waiting for her mother's plane to land, but she began to doze off to sleep as the time approached 1830 hours.

'Beep! Beep!! Beep . . . the alarm clock rang out.

'Why was the alarm set so loud?' asked Susan, who had woken suddenly in Anonsa's house. She hadn't really recovered from the jet lag of her trip from the USA. Her plane had arrived by 1845 hours and she had made her way into the terminal expecting to meet Anonsa, who had promised to wait for her there. But when she reached the terminal with her trolley full of her luggage, Anonsa was nowhere to be found. She made for the nearest telephone booth and called her daughter's cell phone, which was what woke Anonsa up. She had dozed off and was completely unaware of what was going on around her.

'Mummy! Mummy!' Anonsa had exclaimed when she was suddenly jolted awake by the sound of her phone ringing. She sat up and wiped her eyes, looking a bit embarrassed then pressed the answer button on her phone and began speaking to her mum.

'Welcome, mummy! Are you still in the baggage reclaim area? We were told that the flight was delayed.'

'I'm already out in the waiting area. I didn't see you when I came out and I decided to call your phone . . .'

'Mummy, I can see you and I'm walking towards the tele-phone booth where you are,' Anonsa cut in having spotted her mother. Anonsa stood up and almost broke into a run as she moved towards her mother. Susan was now standing outside the phone booth, directly behind her was a lady with her young son who was crying loudly. Susan turned round and saw Anonsa walking towards her. Both of them then ran towards each other

161

and held each other in a tight embrace for almost a whole minute.

'Anonsa, how are you? My lovely and wonderful daughter; looking smart and beautiful as always,' said Susan and tears began to roll down her cheeks.

'Mummy, you are just too sweet. I was so anxious when they announced that your flight was delayed,' said Anonsa and she too started to cry.

Their meetings were usually very emotional whenever they hadn't seen each other for a while. It always reminded Susan of how she and her daughter sat by her husband's hospital bedside when he was dying and Anonsa was only six years old. After their long hug they walked towards Susan's abandoned trolley which was packed with her luggage. Anonsa wheeled the trolley to the taxi rank and both women climbed into the cab after the driver had loaded all the luggage into the boot. They drove to the train station to board a train to Swansea.

'What time did Uncle Sholuston say he will be coming to Swansea?' asked Anonsa. She was watching television in the living room.

'He told me that he will be here by 2.00 p.m. And I trust him, he never arrives late for appointments,' said Susan.

'That's fine.'

'Anonsa, I really like the designs on your duvet cover. It's got so many flowers: roses, carnations and hydrangea. Where did you get it from?' Susan asked as she walked into the kitchen to put the kettle on.

'I bought it from one of the high street stores. I can't remember where exactly.'

Anonsa was lying on the sofa watching one of her favourite

television programmes. Susan did not hear her response as she was already in the kitchen.

'Mum, I forgot to mention, I've been taking Welsh lessons and I'm really enjoying it. At least that should justify my living in a Welsh city . . .'

'Anonsa, I said where did you buy this nice duvet cover?' cut in Susan.

'I already told you that I bought it from one of the high street stores.'

'I was in the kitchen. I did not hear you, so you must have been talking to yourself then.'

Anonsa broke into laughter and Susan joined in. They both had a good sense of humour and they enormously enjoyed each other's company. Her mother joined Anonsa in the living room, while she waited for the kettle to boil.

'Mum, what programme do you want to watch?'

'What time are they showing *Eastenders?*'

'Let's find out.'

Anonsa began to press various buttons on the remote control. 'It's not on today.'

'How about *Prime Minister's Question Time?*'

'No mum, that's only on Wednesdays at midday. I remember you told me that you were a keen politician at school.'

'I really like a good debate, that's why I normally watch it.'

'I can change to another channel for you.'

Susan went into the kitchen to make them both a cup of tea. After a few minutes she came back into the living room carrying a tray with a pair of saucers and two cups of tea which she laid down on the table.

'How about sugar?'

'Mum, I don't take sugar in my tea anymore,' said Anonsa,

chuckling to herself. 'I've been watching my weight since I broke up with Baguda. If I should get out of shape now, few men will bother to look at me and I'd really like to settle down now like Richmond and Peter.'

'Of course I know that you've stopped putting sugar in your tea. I was only teasing you.'

'By the way mum, you haven't told me about your visit to America. I guess that you are keeping the story until Uncle Sholuston comes today.'

'Of course, you guessed right. You know I like my stories to be told to a larger audience, especially when they're red hot from the oven.'

They both started laughing.

'In case I forget, mum, we'll have to go to Tesco later for some shopping – I've run out of a few things.'

'That's fine. Why is it always Tesco, what's wrong with Sainsbury's and Safeway?'

'It's just for the sake of convenience. My friend used to live close to Tesco and whenever I visited her, I'd just do my shopping on my way home. It was just so easy.'

'Anonsa, Richmond's wife was so nice and cute. They really got on very well . . .'

'Mum, you said you were saving the stories until Uncle Sholuston arrives,' Anonsa teased. 'I knew you wouldn't be able to wait that long, that you would definitely start telling a story as soon as you were well rested.'

They both began to giggle.

'Let me finish my story. Paula was really cute and their twin sons Michael and Gregory looked so stunning. I couldn't help being proud to be a grandmother. You know that I had always been nervous about becoming a grandmother, but I never knew that I would enjoy and savour it so much,' said Susan. 'Peter also came with his family from North Carolina and the house was just alive with vivacity and the four kids were running around and enjoying themselves together. Peter's wife, Rebecca, was still breastfeeding. Her father has just been appointed as a judge of the United States Supreme Court and her mum has recently successfully completed her treatment for breast cancer. They are planning a party in October at their family home in Wichita in Kansas where her grandparents still live. Her parents live in Cleveland, Ohio and they want me to attend the events. They hinted that they want you to be there too, but that they hadn't told you yet as they were a bit unsure about whether you could take time out of your busy schedule then.'

'I'm so happy for them. We always speak on the phone. But I haven't actually seen Peter's new son.'

'It's amazing. Life is such a complex thing. Even as you are being struck by tragedy, God blesses you with good things too. I really want to celebrate with them. Having lost my husband to cancer and knowing the difference it would have made had he survived, I can fully appreciate why they want to celebrate.'

'I agree with you, mum. The uncertainty and unpredictability of life can sometimes be unsettling,' Anonsa waxed philosophical 'what about Paula's parents?

'Paula's in constant touch with her parents and they visit her in New York often, though they come separately now that they're divorced.'

'That's nice. At least they still care about their daughter even though their marriage is over.'

'Watch out, the traffic light is changing to red,' shouted Susan, who was seated in the front passenger seat beside Anonsa.

'Don't worry, mum, I'm very alert.'

Anonsa was driving her red, Ford Mondeo along the Camarthen road in Swansea on their way to Tesco.

'There's so much traffic on this road today.'

'It's never usually as busy as this, I think it's because of the music festival being held in Victoria Park today.'

Anonsa applied the brake just before a traffic light which had changed to red. Her mind immediately went to paintings when she saw the car in front of her – a grey Citroen Picasso. 'Mummy, I know you like to go to art galleries. I still remember our visit to the National Gallery in London when you visited the UK about three years ago. Do you remember that painting by Rembrandt which you said you had seen before at the Louvre in Paris?'

'Are you sure that it was a Rembrandt and not a Canaletto?'

'No, mum. I'm definitely sure. It was a Rembrandt. I know that Canaletto is one of your favourite painters. Did you know that his real name was Antonio Giovanni Canal?'

They were now going towards the Dylan Thomas Centre.

'That's interesting. You seem to know a lot about paintings and famous painters.'

'I developed an interest after you took us to the National Museum in Onikan in Lagos, when I was in Secondary School.'

'Do you mean that that visit had such an impact on you? I'm really delighted to hear that. I still remember it too. You suddenly disappeared with Richmond and Peter into one of the stores and I was so worried when I couldn't find the three of you,' said Susan. 'As a matter of fact my favourite painters are Gainsborough, Hogarth, Van Gogh and Canaletto.'

'How about Raphael and Michelangelo? And I didn't even hear you mention Leonardo da Vinci, one of the Great Masters. You seem to prefer the British ones like Hogarth and Gainsborough.'

'It's nothing to do with nationality. It's just what I like. I know everyone talks about Da Vinci's *Mona Lisa* and *The Last Supper*. They are absolutely brilliant paintings, but somehow, he is not among my favourites and I don't know why.'

'Well, mum, my favourites are Picasso, Da Vinci, Raphael, Titian, Rubens, Holbein and Veronese. Their chosen themes seem to appeal to me more than those of the other painters. You know painting is a form of communication of human emotions, just like poetry.'

'H'm! Anonsa, I'm really impressed, shouldn't you enrol in an art school or better still take up a part-time job as a TV commentator on the Arts?' teased Susan. Both women began to laugh.

'That would be fantastic. Mum, that's the Swansea Museum over there and the Leisure Centre is not far away either.'

Anonsa was now at Tesco and she was driving into the car park.

'This car park is huge!' Susan exclaimed. 'Has it ever gotten so busy that you had difficulty getting a parking place?'

'Oh yes, mum, though it's quite rare. The only time I can remember was on a Saturday last August. I remember because I had an appointment with a colleague of mine that day and I was rushing to do a quick shopping and hurry back home only to find there was no where to park. I was about to give up, when an elderly lady drove off, leaving a free space and I quickly drove into it.'

When Anonsa had parked they went into the supermarket and began to buy everything they would need to prepare dinner for Susan's younger brother, Sholuston, whom they were expecting from London that day.

'Anonsa, I hope you haven't forgotten the curry?'

'No, mum. I picked it up while you were getting the bag of rice, that's why you didn't notice it.'

After they finished shopping, Anonsa wheeled their trolley to the counter. There weren't many people queuing up, so within minutes, both women were back in the car again.

'Anonsa, let's avoid that road we came on. Let's take another one that's less busy.'

'Mum, you're a mind reader! That's exactly what I was thinking. Oystermouth Road would be our best bet, it's usually quiet at the weekend. The problem is that sometimes you encounter drunken youths congregating in large numbers there and trying to cause problems for motorists. However, this happens only occasionally. I think we can try it.'

Anonsa drove in the direction of Oystermouth Road.

'You haven't told me about your boyfriend, Baguda,' cut in Susan.

'He's a ex-boyfriend, mum,' Anonsa corrected her. 'We've broken up with each other so he's now part of the past.'

'I'm sorry for the slip. Yes, what about him? What really happened? You know that we've not been able to discuss it yet and I wouldn't want us to talk about it when Sholuston is around because I know that you wouldn't like it.'

'Mum, it's a long story . . .'

'By the way, why do they call him Baguda? It almost sounds like Bagauda Lake in Kano State in Nigeria. Didn't you say that his father was a white British man and his mother, even though she was British-born, was from the Efik tribe in Cross Rivers State in Nigeria?'

'Yes. I don't know the origin of his name but his English name is Theophilus. I met him through a friend of mine at a party when I was working in Dundee. He's actually been very nice.

He was introduced to me by this friend called Theresa with whom I was working at the time. I was not instantly attracted to him even though he was quite good-looking, but he seemed to fancy me as he kept on staring at me during the party before we were finally introduced to each other. I remember he was holding a cigarette at the time and he was smoking in a non-smoking area. I initially thought "h'm, who is this guy?" when suddenly Theresa appeared and introduced him as her friend who worked as a solicitor in a law firm in Dundee. I found him to be intelligent and broad-minded. He seemed to know some-thing about every subject on earth and I thought that he was quite versatile. I was really impressed by him. He was also polite and well-mannered. After the party, he told me that he had enjoyed my company and asked for my telephone number. To cut a long story short, we began seeing each other regularly after-wards.'

Anonsa then paused and tears began to roll down her cheeks. Luckily, she was no longer driving as they had arrived home and had now unloaded their shopping from the car. Susan quickly fetched some tissues for her and she held her close and patted her on the back.

'My daughter, it must have been hard for you. I didn't know all the details before. God will definitely comfort you and give you someone with whom you'll live happily forever.'

'Thank you, mum.'

Susan was sympathetic. They were now sitting together on the sofa in the living room and Anonsa was quite happy to have someone with whom to share her sorrows and emotional pains, which she had been bottling up. She was glad to continue her story even though her mother was a bit worried about her getting so upset.

'Should we postpone the discussion until when you feel a bit better?' asked Susan.

'No mum, I want to continue and get it off my chest.'

'Fine, I'm all ears.'

'Where did I stop?' said Anonsa, after wiping the tears from her eyes. She continued.

'I did not realise early on in the relationship that he was still seeing his former mixed-race girlfriend with whom he told me he had broken up. And as if that was not enough, he also had another affair with a Black South African girl who was an undergraduate at the University of the Witwatersrand in South Africa.'

'How was he able to do all of these things?'

'I'm usually a smart person as you know, mum, but I completely trusted him not knowing that he was a very cunning fellow, though quite charming. He had probably assumed from stories he had heard about the practice of polygamy in Nigeria, that a girl who was brought up there would be tolerant of such behaviour. But he got it wrong completely. He did not realise that I did not belong in that category, even though I was brought up in Nigeria.'

'How did he manage the South African relationship?'

'His father had lived briefly in South Africa in the past and still had business interests there, so he used to accompany his father to South Africa on business trips. I guess that was how he met her. And the last one that led to our final separation . . .' Anonsa looked up at the clock before she continued. 'Mum, the day is going so fast.'

'Do you want to continue the story later on?'

'I'm thinking of my uncle's visit. I'll finish my story later so that we can prepare for Uncle Sholuston and don't disappoint him. You know that he always likes sumptuous entertainment especially this time as he's coming all the way from London.'

'I'm sorry, my daughter. I really empathize with you. Emotional issues are never easy,' said Susan before they both went into the kitchen to prepare meals for their expected guest.

Anonsa joined her mother in the dining room and they both set the table which was covered with a white embroidered table cloth. They put vases with flowers at either end of the table.

'Sholuston should be here at any moment now,' said Susan.

'Mum, let me quickly check my car, I think I left my coat inside it.'

Anonsa went towards the door and opened it. There was her Uncle Sholuston standing outside with his hand raised as though he was just about to press the door bell.

'Hey! Uncle, welcome,' exclaimed Anonsa and she rushed to embrace him.

'How are you, Pelu?' said Sholuston.

'I'm doing fine. I see you still like to call me by my Yoruba name.'

They both went inside the house. They were delighted to see each other even though they spoke regularly by phone.

'Sholu, how are you? We've been waiting expectantly and I knew that you'd definitely arrive on time. I'm happy to see you,' said Susan as she rose up to hug her brother.

'Uncle, did you come via the M4?'

'No. I changed my mind and came by train from Cardiff, as I had to go to the University there to see my supervisor about my PhD thesis. We were together longer than I had anticipated and we ended up finishing our discussions at 6.30 p.m., so I had no choice but to put up at a hotel for the night before boarding a train for Swansea this morning,' said Sholuston. 'That's why I shifted the time to 2 p.m. today.'

'You must be tired then,' said Anonsa as she fetched some bottled water from the refrigerator and poured a glass for Sholuston, who was now seated on the sofa in the living room.

'No, I'm actually refreshed, because I slept well,' said Sholuston. 'My lovely sister, how was your trip? I . . .'

'Shrrh! Shrrh!! Shrrh!!! . . .'

Sholuston was interrupted by the telephone ringing.

'Excuse me, Uncle,' said Anonsa as she made a dash to pick up the phone.

'Hello?' said Anonsa.

'Hello, Anonsa . . .' came the response from the other end.

'Ah Richmond, are you clairvoyant or telepathic? How did you know that Uncle Sholuston is here? He's just arrived and mum is still here too. We are all about to start eating and you are welcome to join us,' said Anonsa and she began to laugh.

'How nice. I think I can even smell the food. Wouldn't it be marvellous for me to dash onto the next available plane and land on your doorstep?' teased Richmond.

'Never mind, if only we had a plane that travelled at the speed of light. Who knows, it might be possible in a hundred years' time if mankind continues, with its current rate of technological advancement,' said Anonsa.

'That would be amazing. Let me speak to Uncle Sholuston and then Mum.'

'OK, hold on . . .'

Anonsa walked towards her uncle's seat carrying the phone and tapped him gently on the shoulder. 'Uncle, it's Richmond calling from America he wants to speak to you,' she said, handing over the phone and joining her mum in the kitchen to help serve the meals.

'Richy,' exclaimed Sholuston, 'It's almost unbelievable. How are you? Are you a mind reader? I've only just arrived here to see Susan and I was just going to ask after you when the telephone suddenly started ringing. I'm really delighted to speak to you.'

'I'm really happy to speak to you too, Uncle. It's been so difficult to track you down. Everytime I called, you were always out and whenever you called I didn't seem to be around either,' said Richmond.

'That's quite true. How's your family? And how about Peter and his family too? Your mum just told me that he came with his wife and kids to New York to see her. I think that was very kind of him.'

'We are all doing fine. Peter has gone back to Raleigh with his family now and they phoned me after they had arrived home. His wife's parents are planning a Thanksgiving party in October and I'm sure they'll want you to be there, even though they haven't let you know about it yet.'

'Are you letting me into a secret?' teased Sholuston.

'Something like that and also to sound you out on their behalf,' said Richmond.

They both started laughing.

'When are you coming to Britain to visit us again? Sylvia and Jake are dying to see you.'

'Uncle, I'll have to plan it well, because at the moment we are really busy. Some of my partners are currently on leave and there's so much work to do. But Peter hopes to come to Britain in a few months' time and he definitely intends to visit you, even though he's going to be there on business,' said Richmond.

'That'll be fantastic.'

'When next I visit London, I hope to go around the art galleries. Are there any other places you can recommend where

I can see lovely paintings apart from Tate Britain and the National Gallery?'

'A tour of the Historic Palaces would be a good idea as well as Buckingham Palace, if you come in the summertime. And, as for paintings, have you ever been to the Queen's gallery?'

'No.'

'I think it would be nice to incorporate it into your tour of the State Rooms and the Royal Mews.'

'Oh, the Royal Mews! I've heard a lot about it. Mum and Anonsa used to talk about it. If I'm right, I think that's where they have all those golden carriages that the Queen and members of the royal family normally use for ceremonial occasions?'

'Yes, you are right.'

'I'd really love to go there when next I come to London. Thanks, Uncle, you must be hungry by now so let me have a quick word with Mum, before I say goodbye. I'm really over the moon to be able to speak to you. I'll keep on phoning regularly.'

'It's been marvellous talking to you. Hold on while I hand over the phone to your mum . . .'

Sholuston looked over his shoulder and saw Susan walking towards him. He beckoned to her to take the phone.

'Richy, my darling son. It's thrilling for all three of us to be able to speak to you,' said Susan.

'Mum, how was your journey? You were sleeping when I called earlier on to find out if you had arrived safely,' said Richmond.

'Anonsa told me you had called. The journey was delayed, however, when we eventually left, it was very smooth and pleasant.'

'I'm happy to hear that you had a smooth trip,' said Richmond. 'Peter has gone back to Raleigh with his family. I spoke to him just after he arrived.'

'That's very kind of you. I'm really proud of both of you and

Anonsa too. I consider myself very lucky to have you all as my children. You give me plenty of affection and support, and it has made me to be able to cope with your dad's absence from our lives all this while,' said Susan, trying to hold back tears.

'Mum, we are all flattered by your praise. I think we should all be grateful to you for your love and steadfastness in the face of the difficulties we faced after we lost our dad. You were able to send us to university and now we are all independent and Peter and I have families of our own. I pray that Anonsa's time will soon come and she too will be settled with a nice husband and kids. What more can we ask for in life? Mum, you are one in a million. May God continue to strengthen the love between all of us forever.'

Tears were now rolling down Richmond's cheeks as he spoke.

'Richy, you are so kind. God will answer your prayer.'

'Mum, you must be hungry now. We'll speak again very soon. Let me leave you to join uncle and Anonsa at the table and enjoy your meal. *Bon appetit.*'

'Thank you. Goodbye.'

After hanging up Susan dried her tears and went to join Sholuston and Anonsa at the table.

'Are you all set and raring to go?' teased Susan as she joined them.

'You know that I'm the current world record holder for gluttony,' joked Sholuston.

'Yes, I can see that's why you have such a large frame,' said Susan and all three of them laughed at the irony of this as Sholuston was a slim man with a svelte figure. They all immediately descended on the meal which included Nigerian dishes: pounded yam with *egusi* soup and beef; fried rice and *dodo* with mixed vegetable salad and orange and apple juice. There was also ice-cream and other desserts.

'This food is delicious,' complimented Sholuston.

'Thank you, Uncle,' replied Anonsa who was delighted by the compliment.

'How about this PhD thesis you were talking about?' asked Susan.

'It's been on-going for some years now. I want to finish it this year. It's a part-time course,' replied Sholuston, as he helped himself to another glass of orange juice. Sholuston had graduated in marine biology from the University of Liverpool and proceeded to do a masters degree in fisheries at the University of Edinburgh, before he started working with a company that imported aquatic materials.

'Anonsa, I hope you are enjoying your current job in public health. I remember you told me that you had always loved public health as a specialty. Is there any reason in particular?' asked Sholuston.

'I just like to work with the people in the community instead of in the restrictive atmosphere of a hospital setting – though I did enjoy my work as a senior house officer in the hospital.'

'I just feel that you doctors work too hard for little pay,' said Sholuston.

'You are right. It used to be worse, but the European Union is now aware of the negative impact on doctors' health of excessive workloads and they have done something about it. We now have a maximum number of hours per week beyond which we are not legally allowed to work. Though, some health authorities still flout this rule when they are very short staffed,' said Anonsa. 'It has really made life better for us. Now we have time to attend to things in our lives which other people take for granted and which in the past was almost impossible for us.'

'That's quite an improvement then,' said Sholuston.

'Absolutely. Mum, could you please pass me that bottle of water,' requested Anonsa as she reached out for more salad.

'Thank you, mum,' said Anonsa as she poured the water into her glass.

'Taran ra taran rarara! Taran ra taran rara . . .' came a sound from the corner of the room.

'Where's that music coming from?' queried Susan.

'It's my mobile phone ringing,' said Sholuston as he got up to get his phone from his coat pocket.

'Hello, Sylvia, how are you? I'm in Swansea now. In fact, I'm having dinner with Susan and Anonsa. I'll be back in London tomorrow.'

'Daddy, we are missing you,' said Sylvia, who was Sholuston's teenaged daughter.

'I know that. Has your mummy returned from the gym?'

'No. She told me that she'll be going to Sainsbury's for some shopping after leaving the gym. You can call her on her mobile,' said Sylvia.

'We've spoken to each other already today. I'll pass you over to your Aunt,' said Sholuston as he handed the phone to Susan, who was wiping her hands on a towel.

'Sylvia, how are you?' asked Susan delightedly.

'Aunty, I'm doing fine. When are you coming to see us in London?'

'I'll be over next week. I wanted to come earlier but your daddy insisted on coming to see me in Swansea first. Don't worry, I'll definitely see all of you when I come.'

'How about Anonsa?'

'Hold on,' said Susan as she handed the phone over to Anonsa, who was already looking excited at the prospect of speaking to her young cousin.

'Sylvia, how are you?' said Anonsa.

'I'm doing fine.'

'Have you carried out the assignment that I gave you when we last spoke?' Anonsa giggled.

'Yes of course, I've done it.'

'So we'll talk about it when I come to London with mummy next week.'

'Do you mean that you're coming to London with aunty too?'

'Yes.'

'I can't wait to see you!'

'Let me hand you over to your daddy. Goodbye until next week,' ended Anonsa as she walked towards Sholuston to hand him the phone.

'Sylvia, goodbye until tomorrow,' said Sholuston.

'Goodnight daddy. Make sure you sleep well.'

'I'll try,' replied Sholuston before Sylvia hung up.

By the time dinner was finished it was about 9 o'clock. Sholuston retired to bed after taking a shower while Anonsa and Susan were watching a documentary on Queen Victoria.

'It's unbelievable that she came to the throne at the tender age of eighteen,' said Susan. 'And she ended up becoming the longest-ruling monarch in the history of the British monarchy, with many descendants spread among most of Europe's royal families.'

'That's life and destiny. I believe that she was destined to do that,' said Anonsa who was not very conversant with the history of the British monarchy.

'Mum, I really like this biography channel, I'm learning so much that I didn't know before about many important historical figures.'

'I enjoy watching it myself, even though we studied bits of British history during my undergraduate years at Harvard, this channel helps to refresh my memory and also fill in some gaps in my knowledge.'

Susan then began to scan through the other channels as the programme came to an end.

'Mum, I need to go to bed now so that I can drive uncle to the train station tomorrow.'

'That's fine.'

Sholuston was already fast asleep in his room.

'Good night, mum,' said Anonsa as she went into her bedroom.

'Good night and I'll see you tomorrow,' said Susan.

Susan stayed in the sitting room watching the programmes on TV.

She then began to think of the new man in her life from Okene in Nigeria. His name was Onimisi. She had met him during a trip to attend a dental conference in Paris about ten months earlier. After a while she switched off the TV and went to bed.

15

Susan was driving into her mansion in the Government Reservation Area in Ilorin, after a trip to Abuja to see the new man in her life, Onimisi Anate. She had spent a week with him in the Asokoro Area, where he lived. She had arrived back from the UK about four weeks earlier, where she visited her daughter, Anonsa, and her younger brother, Sholuston, and his family. Having also visited her sons, a cousin and friends in the USA she felt satisfied with her trip.

Susan had refused to get involved with any man since she lost her husband many years before. She had been so devastated by his death, which happened when her children were still very young, that she vowed not to marry again. She became completely devoted to her children. When she cast her mind back, she felt no regret at all for her decision but her children were now all grown up.

She first met Onimisi in Paris by chance while she was attending a dental conference. He was representing Nigeria at a conference of diplomats, which was held under the auspices of the United Nations.

Susan had been at the Gare du Nord and being a non-French speaker, she was looking for English language newspapers and magazines to buy. She eventually saw a copy of *Newsweek* in one of the shops at the station and she promptly went to get it. After picking up the only copy she noticed that a black man standing near by had been about to reach for it too. She glanced at the man after paying and when their eyes met, he smiled at her. She suspected that he might be Nigerian judging by the traditional dress he wore. She, on the other hand, was wearing a smart white suit. Susan was ebony-complexioned and of average height, while Onimisi was quite tall and of very light brown complexion.

'Hello, it seems as if you were interested in the *Newsweek* magazine too. I'm sorry, I picked it up before you did,' said Susan.

'It's all right,' said Onimisi.

'May I ask if you are from Nigeria?' said Susan, and she smiled.

'Yes, I'm from Nigeria. How about you?'

'I'm from Nigeria too.'

They shook hands and exchanged pleasantries, then walked together to the Rue La Fayette, talking about many things. The venue for Susan's conference was not far from the station. She was staying at the Concorde La Fayette Hotel and was due to travel back to Nigeria by Air France the following day. Onimisi had put up at the Edouard VII Hotel and he had yet to attend his own conference, which was still two days away. They chatted happily for a few hours while looking round Paris together and after visiting the Eiffel Tower, they eventually parted company. But they made a point of exchanging their phone numbers and promised to get in touch when they were both back in Nigeria.

Susan and Onimisi didn't see each other again until one day when Onimisi, who worked at the Ministry of Foreign Affairs in

Abuja, was told by his secretary that a lady wanted to see him. He asked his secretary to let her in and Susan opened the office door little suspecting who awaited her inside. They were both completely startled and pleasantly surprised. Susan hugged him and they both apologized for not contacting each other. Susan realized immediately that she could not keep her vow of not getting involved with any man much longer. They were both smitten with each other. She had actually come to process her nomination to attend a Women's Conference in Santiago, as part of the Nigerian delegation, and it so happened that Onimisi was in charge of organizing the conference.

When Susan got back from Chile they began to spend time together. Onimisi did most of the travelling initially, but Susan started to visit him more often when the relationship became more established. She was happy to have found someone she truly loved again.

Onimisi was from Okene in Kogi State and he was Ebira by origin. He was about three years older than Susan and had studied sociology at the University of Ibadan. After graduation, he joined the Nigerian Army and was sent to the Royal Military Academy in Sandhurst for training. A few years after returning to Nigeria, he was discharged from the army on health grounds after sustaining an injury during a mountaineering expedition. He then joined the Ministry of Foreign Affairs and was sent to do a Masters in international relations at the University of Edinburgh. Afterwards he went to Oxford to do a PhD degree before returning to Nigeria to work at the Ministry of Foreign Affairs.

Onimisi had two children who were living and working in London. His wife had died of complications during surgery many years before and he had refused to remarry afterwards, though he had had a string of affairs with some glamorous women, before he met Susan.

Susan was from Ilorin in Kwara State and she was Yoruba by origin. When she left school she won a scholarship to study dentistry at Harvard University and, after qualifying, she returned to Nigeria, where she met her husband.

Susan and Onimisi were very happy together. She eventually told her children and other members of her family, after initially keeping their relationship secret. She was surprised to have fallen in love again. She told herself that love must be like a ruptured dam that swept everything in its path, otherwise she was at a loss to explain the instantaneous melting of her long-kept vow after meeting Onimisi.

Susan woke up the following morning and was ready to go to her clinic, which adjoined her house, when she had a phone call from her friend Dupe, who was living in Ibadan. Dupe told her that she was on her way to see her about an urgent matter, which she refused to disclose over the phone. Susan was a bit worried and she wondered what the issue could be that Dupe could not even broach over the phone. She knew too, that Dupe could sometimes make a mountain out of a mole hill by exaggerating the importance of little things. They had both attended Queen Elizabeth School in Ilorin. Dupe then went on to study political science at the University of Ibadan, and Susan remembered how she used to joke whenever they spoke to each other, saying 'I moved from Queen to Queen.' This was because she stayed in Queen Elizabeth II Hall of residence at University, after finishing her A Levels at Queen Elizabeth School. Dupe even became known among her friends as 'Queen to Queen' and she really loved it. Susan began to wonder whether the urgent matter had anything to do with Dupe's daughter, who was due to get married in a fortnight.

After arriving at the clinic, however, Susan focused on her work and luckily for her it was a very busy day with so many patients to see that she had virtually no time to ruminate over Dupe's phone call. She had already scheduled a meeting with her staff at 1.30 p.m. and was also due to attend a gala dinner that night in Government House. The day was particularly hot, which made her drink large quantities of water. At the staff meeting she was able to review many of the decisions which had been made in her absence. Her practice was thriving and she had retainerships with many companies. She also had plenty of investments in companies and properties in Ilorin and Lagos. Her staff all enjoyed working with her and they were well remunerated. After the meeting she went home for a siesta. When she eventually woke up, she saw a text message from Dupe explaining that the reason she wanted to see Susan was because of her daughter's forth-coming wedding. She then made a phone call to her sister who was a lecturer in the University of Jos, but she was not at home. The phone call was answered by her guest, Patience, a childhood friend who happened to have just entered the house when the phone rang.

'Hello, who's on the line?'

'It's Susan. May I speak to Veronica please?'

'Hi, Susan!' exclaimed Patience. 'It's quite some time since we've seen or spoken to each other. I've just arrived at Veronica's house. I'm in Jos for a two-week course at the university, so I decided to stay with Veronica. How was your trip abroad?'

'Hi, Patience. It's so nice to hear your voice again. Thank you. My trip was very successful. How's your husband?'

'He's doing fine. He was recently promoted and we are all very happy for him. Veronica told me that you've got a new man in your life and I was really happy to hear that.'

'That's true. I'm back on the love train again and I think I like it. The man is Ebira by origin and he is from Okene.'

'That's interesting. My husband is Igala, which means that they are from the same State, Kogi.'

'Yes. Onimisi is lovely and an absolute lion in bed,' said Susan, and they both giggled. 'I ran into your elder sister in Abuja about four months ago and she told me that she now works in the Union Bank there and that her husband is a consultant orthopaedic surgeon at the National Orthopaedic Hospital in Lagos. How's that all working out?'

'I guess they'll cope. They are working at it. Luckily for her, her job involves travelling a lot. Sometimes she can be in Lagos for up to three weeks at a time. Her husband travels to Abuja too, especially at weekends. Their children are all grown up now.'

'That's nice. Well Patience, I think I should leave you to rest. I hope your course is successful. Please tell Veronica that I'll phone her again, but I'm going to a gala dinner at Government House tonight.'

'It's been so nice to speak to you. Have a pleasant outing. I'll pass on your message to Veronica when she comes back,' said Patience and she put down the telephone receiver.

Susan was driven to Government House that evening by her chauffeur. When they arrived at the gates, they had to undergo routine security checks before they were allowed inside the compound. Her driver parked and then accompanied her to the entrance.

Susan was wearing a traditional costume of a blouse and wrapper, and elaborate head gear. On entering the hall where the event was taking place, she met other guests some of whom had travelled from far and wide. There were state commissioners, top government officials, and business executives. The guests moved around in droves and introduced themselves to one another with lots of handshakes and exchanges of banter. The venue was big and brightly lit, with lots of decorations. A few minutes after Susan had entered the hall, she was greeted by an usherette and as she turned round, she spotted an old classmate, Bunmi, from the Queen Elizabeth School. They had not seen each other since they finished their A Levels.

'Hello Bunmi,' said Susan as she walked towards her.

'Hello Susan. It's been such a long time,' said Bunmi as they rushed to embrace. They were both excited to see each other.

'How are you? It has been a long time, hasn't it? You've changed a lot. I hardly recognized you when I saw you,' said Susan.

Bunmi used to be very slim when they were at school, but she had put on weight from having children.

'*You* haven't changed much,' said Bunmi. 'You look as young as ever. But tell me, how did you enjoy studying in America?'

'Very much, thank you. But I left America a long time ago.'

'And what have you been doing? I know that you are now a dentist.'

'After I qualified and returned from America, I got married to a civil engineer from Offa and we had three children. I started my private practice here in Ilorin after working for some years at the Dental Centre at the University College Hospital in Ibadan. But unfortunately, my husband died a long time ago. I was in private practice when he died and I'm still doing that now. You are now Mrs . . .'

'I'm Mrs Danladi. After we left school, I went to Ahmadu Bello University in Zaria to study botany, and after working at the

Yankari Game Reserve for a few years, I came back to do a Masters degree. It was in Zaria that I met my husband. He studied architecture. We have four children. I've joined him in Zaria where we both lecture now.'

'Have you travelled all the way from Zaria today?'

'No. My mother-in-law is from Ilorin. I came to visit her and have been in town for a few days. The governor's wife is my friend, so when she found out that I was in town, she decided to invite me to this gala evening. That's why I'm here tonight. My husband is still in Zaria.'

'That's interesting.'

They were interrupted by a young man who came to deliver a message to Bunmi.

'Susan, excuse me for a minute. It seems I'm needed, but I'll join you shortly,' said Bunmi, as she was led away by the young man.

Susan later joined a group of acquaintances, and also met many other people whom she had come to know over the years, though none of them went to school with her apart from Bunmi. She began to reminisce about her time at the Queen Elizabeth School. She remembered an incident that happened when she was a House Prefect, when two girls were caught in bed together and the incident became a scandal. Some students had reported them to the school authorities, claiming that they were fondling each other, but the students involved denied ever doing such a thing. She had handled the matter in a very tactful manner at the time. She remembered that those girls later suffered the humiliation of being nicknamed by their schoolmates. They were called 'in bed' throughout their time at the school. This event had enabled her to be more tolerant and understanding when decades later her own daughter, Anonsa, was caught in the toilet with a boy.

She also remembered her French teacher who was from Lome in Togo, and her chemistry teacher, who was a British woman from Plymouth. They had both been very nice to her. She remembered being invited to dinner in the staff quarters by the chemistry teacher and her husband, who was from Belfast. He taught mathematics at the school. He tried to explain the sectarian crisis in Northern Ireland to her and she used to listen sympathetically, even though she could not fully grasp the intricacies of the situation and its origins.

Susan had been at the event for about an hour and had seen nearly everyone she knew, including the governor's wife, when an announcement was made that the guests should proceed to the main hall. She had no idea that good news awaited her. The invitation she had received had mentioned the two-year anniversary of the governor's rule and she thought that was why she had been invited. As she climbed the steps, somebody tapped her on the shoulder and told her that the governor wanted to see her urgently before she went into the hall. Looking startled, Susan accompanied the young lady to one of the offices where the governor was waiting for her.

'Good evening, Mrs Omiyale,' said the governor, as he got up to shake her hand. 'Please take a seat.'

'Thank you,' said Susan and she sat down.

'I just wanted to congratulate you on your appointment as the new Commissioner for Health.' The governor proceeded to hand over a letter to her.

Susan was flabbergasted. She broke down in tears and managed to utter feebly, 'Thank you, your Excellency. I'm just lost for words.'

After wiping her tears, she gathered herself together.

She had been aware that she might be considered for the post of Commissioner for Health, with the impending retirement of current Commissioner, but she had not expected the news that night.

'Is there anything that you'd like to say, before we reveal even more surprises and tell you why you weren't informed before-hand?'

Susan, who was normally eloquent, could not find anything to say.

'I really don't know what to say, other than to thank you for the honour which you've bestowed on me.'

Susan had always loved public duty, and now that she had four capable dentists working for her, she knew that she did not have anything to fear in terms of the effect of her new appointment on her thriving practice. After thanking the governor, she went out to join the other guests, while she awaited the next round of surprises. When she got into the hall, she was seated in a place that had been reserved for her. She began to think about what else was going to be revealed and to wonder why everything had been kept secret from her. Her mind momentarily wandered to Onimisi, but he had told her that he would be in Lagos that evening attending a function.

About thirty minutes later, the event started. The Master of Ceremonies made the introductions which were followed by the presentation of medals of long service to some people who were retiring. They all received rapturous applause when they were individually called to receive them. Then Susan's name was announced for an award for her tireless contribution to the improvement of the dental health of the people, and she was presented with a plaque by the governor. Her appointment as a Commissioner was also announced. The hall came to a near standstill, as she received a thunderous standing ovation. As Susan took the microphone to give her acceptance speech, she came face to face with Onimisi, who was standing there dressed in a flowing traditional costume and a matching cap. She rushed to embrace him and tears started rolling down her cheeks again while the audience gave them a big round of applause. After embracing Onimisi, she calmed down and took the microphone to begin her speech.

'I must first start by thanking the governor, for giving me this wonderful opportunity to serve my State and also for the award,' she said. 'Saying that I'm overwhelmed with joy would be a gross understatement. I'm indeed exceedingly delighted to be given these double honours tonight. Firstly, for rendering dental services to the people and secondly to begin to serve. There is a link between both of them, and it is that of continuity of service. I am standing on the podium of history tonight, as the first woman to receive this award and that in itself fills me with special joy, that the achievements of women are being duly recognized in this important way. I trust in God and in the hard work of our women, and I promise to serve to the best of my ability, in my new capacity as the Commissioner for Health. I dedicate this service award to women in all the professions and also to all those who work very hard to look after their families but who remain in oblivion. The family is the unit and building block of any society. My thanks also go to my partner, Onimisi, my late husband, children, parents, siblings, relatives and friends who have contributed immeasurably to my success in life. Thank you all.'

As she finished her speech and went back to her seat, tumultuous applause rang through the hall. After the meal was over, many people came to her to congratulate Susan as she and Onimisi walked out of the hall together to join her driver, who was already waiting in the car. They hugged and kissed each other with joy.

'Darling, I love you with all my heart. I want to be with you forever so that I can continue to shower you with my affection. How did you manage to keep this secret?' said Susan as she sat down in the car.

'Honey, I'll soon tell you. My love is yours forever and you deserve every bit of it,' said Onimisi, as the driver started the car and drove off towards Susan's home.

'What a lovely surprise it was to see you. When did you arrive and where have you been hiding?'

'I actually arrived today and I was holed up in the Kwara Hotel in order to avoid running into you or anyone who might inform you that they had seen me, and spoil the surprise.'

'When the governor told me that I'd soon know why the whole thing was kept secret from me, I was at a loss, until I saw you and everything clicked.'

'I asked him to make it a surprise package for you after I found out, and he agreed, being an easy going man and also a personal friend.'

The driver was now approaching Susan's house.

'That was an elaborate plan.'

As they finally arrived at her house, the gate man opened the gates for the car and the driver drove inside the compound and pulled up at the garage. Susan and Onimisi got out of the car and went into the house. As soon as they were inside they went straight to Susan's bedroom and undressed, then went and had a bath together. Afterwards they went into the bedroom where Onimisi slipped into his dressing gown and Susan put on her transparent nightdress. They both climbed into bed and began caressing each other before they made passionate love. As Onimisi thrusted powerfully inside her, Susan filled the room with screams and moans of pleasure. After their energetic love-making session, they lay there together in bed, exhausted, before they finally drifted off to sleep.

Susan and Onimisi woke up on the following morning and, while they were still lying in bed, Susan switched on the TV. They watched the BBC World News before she switched to the Sky News Channel, which was showing people climbing the Eiffel Tower in Paris.

'That reminds me of our time in Paris together. You haven't told me why you always stay at the Edouard VII Hotel whenever you visit Paris,' said Susan.

'Oh, you remember? You medics do seem to remember things. The reason why I stay there whenever I visit Paris is because I was told by the hotel staff that King Edward VII of Great Britain used to stay there when he was the Prince of Wales. Being someone who is interested in Queen Victoria and Prince Albert, I became sentimentally attached to the hotel. Did you know that Edward VII was their eldest son?'

'That's interesting. I didn't realize that. You seem to be quite knowledgeable about the history of British Royalty. Is it anything to do with your Sandhurst training?'

'It's more than that. In total, I lived in Britain for over six years. Apart from the years I spent in Sandhurst, I went back to pursue my Masters and PhD and some of my coursework entailed digging into British history and the history of the monarchy.'

'Do you know anything about Nelson? They were planning to celebrate the two hundredth anniversary of his victory at the Battle of Trafalgar.'

'Yes. Horatio Nelson was a naval commander who led Britain

to victory at the Battle of Trafalgar, losing his life in the process.'

'So much for military history.'

'World security and the burden of maintaining peace fall squarely on the shoulders of the military, and the military has to be fit to be an effective fighting machine.'

'I know that you were an army man, but I had always seen the navy as a more peaceful arm of the Armed Forces until the outbreak of the Falklands War. I really liked their white uniforms. One of my distant cousins was in the Nigerian Navy and he used to tell us stories about it. But I don't really like wars.'

'Nobody likes wars, not even the soldiers whose job is to fight in them. But some wars are inevitable if nations are to defend their freedom from tyranny and oppression, and secure the liberties and rights of the individual in a democratic society. Otherwise, people like Hitler would have been ruling the world by now.'

'I think I agree with you.'

'Thank you.'

'Onimisi, I wanted to ask your opinion about something. I've been invited to become one of the patrons of the Nigerian Chapter of a charity organization but I'm already involved with many other charities, so I don't know whether to accept the offer. Though I do like this particular charity because it carries out work with young people.'

'I think it's an issue of time management. Now that you've been appointed a Commissioner, you may not have the time but my opinion is that you should accept the offer since you like the work which the charity does. But let them know about your commitments.'

'My appointment hasn't really sunk in yet. I'll take your advice. Two heads are better than one, as the saying goes,' said Susan and she burst out laughing.

'I think I'll start to address you as "Madam Commissioner" from now on so that it can sink in quickly,' joked Onimisi. Onimisi had to return to Lagos later in that day before flying on to Abuja, so after a shower and breakfast he started to get ready to leave.

16

Anonsa was sitting cross-legged on the sofa in her sitting room in Swansea. It was over six months since she had split up with Baguda. Following their holiday in Dublin which turned sour, her contract of employment with Ninewells Hospital in Dundee also expired. So she moved to London to stay with her uncle Sholuston and his family. Luckily she had had a successful interview for a specialist registrar job, which was the job she was now doing.

After her brief stay in London she had gone to Nigeria to visit her mother. The trip provided her with emotional and psychological succour. It was when she was returning to London after the visit that she ran into Burnty at Heathrow Airport. They hadn't seen each other since they had both been expelled from High School in Ilorin over a decade earlier. It was an amazing surprise when they met again. Since then they had gone out for dinner in London and it seemed that their love was re-igniting. She was not too sure whether this was due to the fact that they had both broken up with their respective partners. On the few occasions when they went out together, she had noticed that the

195

feeling of fondness between them seemed to be mutual. They also spoke frequently on the phone. Burnty was gradually recovering from his heartbreak and she was helping him on the path to recovery. The impact of the break-up with their respective partners seemed to have destabilized him more than it had her. For now, she was focusing on getting on with her life. She and Burnty had a lot of catching up to do. She told herself that life was full of ups and downs as she tried to put Baguda out of her mind over the last few months. She also thought about how different things might have been had she not been able to leave Dundee.

Her new job helped to cushion the pain she had felt when her relationship with Baguda ended. She reasoned that Burnty's inability to secure a specialist registrar job soon after Emily left him might have exacerbated his own feelings of misery. She realized herself that in the present day, as important as a love life was, it was also vital to have a career with which one was quite satisfied. After her outings with Burnty, something somewhere in her heart kept telling her that she had finally found the man for her. However, she wanted events to take their course naturally. Anonsa went for a shower and got dressed then went downstairs into the sitting room and dialled one of her friend's telephone numbers.

'Hello, this is Letitia Vincenzo,' came the voice from the other end of the line.

'Hi Letitia, it's Anonsa. How are you?'

'Hi Anonsa, it's nice to hear your voice again. I'm doing fine. How are you?' exclaimed Letitia in surprise.

'I'm fine too. I just thought that I'd call and say hello.'

'Thank you for being so thoughtful. It's quite some time now since we've spoken to each other. I believe you are still in Swansea?'

'Yes I am. Are you still working in the Royal Shrewsbury Hospital?'

'Yes I am, and I also go to the hospitals in Telford and Oswestry occasionally. But I'm mainly based in Shrewsbury.'

'I've never been to Shrewsbury but my young cousin in London who's studying for her A Levels once told me that Charles Darwin was born there.'

'Really? I didn't know myself that the great English evolutionist behind the theory of Natural Selection was born in the town where I've been working for over two years. That should inspire me!' said Letitia and she and Anonsa burst out laughing.

'How are your parents?'

'They've gone to Venice to see my grandfather, but they are doing fine, thank you for asking. And how's your mum doing?'

'I spoke to her yesterday. She was well. She told me that she had just finished with the Annual Youth Event for a charity of which she's a patroness. The event was held in Lagos.'

'Was it The Homij And Tanassah Foundation for World Peace?'

'Yes, how did you know that?' Anonsa was gobsmacked.

'The event was shown on CNN and I remembered it because of its acronym. It was called THAT Foundation, which really appealed to me. It had an international outlook, with all the young people attending it representing the different continents of the world. I was impressed by what I saw. Being a member of Amnesty International myself, I liked the idea of teaching people early in life about the virtues of tolerance and peaceful coexistence without consideration of race, religion or place of origin. These values are the ingredients of what we normally preach as human rights in AI. I never knew that the event had anything to do with your mum, though. I'm happy to know that now.'

'I'm totally amazed. I've only ever thought of you as a radiologist, I never knew that you were interested in things like human rights too.'

'It's just one of those activities which I've been involved in since I was an undergraduate.'

'That's great. It's so nice to speak to you. I'll call you again sometime. I've really enjoyed our conversation today.'

'I think I owe you the next call. Sorry not to have called you but I'm the only specialist registrar about just now, the others are either in Telford, Oswestry or on leave.'

'I understand,' said Anonsa as they ended the conversation.

Letitia was one of the people she had met during an Adult Life Support course held in Cardiff many months earlier.

Anonsa had just opened the door to her house, and had barely stepped inside when her cell phone rang. She clumsily tried to take it out of her handbag but it fell on the ground, and as she hurried to pick it up it stopped ringing. As she was about to drop it back into her handbag again, the phone rang again.

'Hello, this is Anonsa. Who's calling?'

She was breathing heavily as if she had just run up a mountain.

'It's Richmond from Copenhagen,' came her brother's response.

'Hi Richy! What are you doing in Copenhagen?' asked Anonsa in surprise.

'Paula and I and the kids have joined her mum for a vacation here. Her mum was here to attend an international conference of architects last week and we stayed on to have some fun.'

'That's interesting. Where are you all staying?'

'The conference was held at the Hotel d'Angleterre in Kongen Nytorv and that's where we are staying.'

'What's the meaning of *Kongen*?'

'It means "King" in Danish.'

'So you've already managed to learn some Danish, that's impressive!'

'Let me show off some more.'

'Fine. Go on.'

'Hvordan har du det?'

'What does that mean?'

'It simply means, "how are you?"'

'And what should I say?'

'You say *"jeg har det godt"*, which means "I'm doing fine".'

'Hm! What a curious language. I know that you are always excited learning new languages. Where have you visited in Denmark so far?'

'We've been to Klampenborg Beach, Tivoli, Magazin du Nord, Radhusplasen and Stroget.'

'How about *Folketinget*, the Danish House of Parliament and Amalienborg Palace?'

'We haven't been to those yet. We've just got back today from Jutland where we visited Arrhus and Kolding. We also passed through Odense on our way back to Copenhagen.'

'That's impressive. I hope the kids are enjoying it too? The only time I've been to Copenhagen was on holiday a few years ago, when I also travelled to Aalborg to see a friend.'

'The kids are having a great time. They've already told me that they want to come back.'

'And they haven't even been to Legoland yet. Maybe they'll refuse to leave Denmark when they've been there,' said Anonsa laughing.

'I don't think that we'll be able to take them there this time around.'

'When are you all returning to the USA?'

'The day after tomorrow.'

'Make the most of your last few days then. I wish you all a safe journey home. I'll phone you when you get back. Give my love to Paula, her mum and the kids.'

'I'll do that. Stay blessed. Goodbye,' said Richmond and then he hung up.

17

Emily and Richard were on the M1 travelling from Nottingham
back to Leicester after a weekend trip. They had gone to check
out Richard's newly opened Fitness Centre in Nottingham. His
business was thriving. They were chatting heartily as Emily
munched a burger. It had been over four months since Emily
moved in with Richard and the house she had shared with Burnty
was up for sale. Her father had been ecstatic when he found out
that she had left Burnty, but her mother and sisters had been
neutral about the whole matter. They believed that it was her
own life and she was the only person who could decide who she
wanted to be with. All that they could do was support her.

Richard had been extremely happy to have Emily move in
with him. It meant that their relationship was now on a formal
basis and the time of clandestine meetings and stolen sex was
over. Now that they lived together, they could make love as
frequently as they wanted to.

'We'll soon be in Leicester,' said Richard, as he glanced at a
road sign saying that the city was only ten miles away.

201

'That's great,' said Emily.

Richard had been in the habit of driving Emily to and from work at Glenfield Hospital, as if to warn any would-be rival that he was her man. He enjoyed this task even though sometimes Emily would have preferred to drive herself to work. He adored her and Emily loved him too, especially since her father approved of their relationship. Even though their love affair was intense, they had no intention of rushing into marriage yet. They were prepared to have children together without necessarily tying the nuptial knot. As they arrived in Leicester, Richard drove into a petrol station to fill up his fuel tank. As he pulled up behind a black, Ford Mondeo, Emily spotted a billboard which had an inscription on it that read: '*LOVE CAN BE ETERNAL, BUT DON'T LOSE YOUR MIND*'. Emily directed Richard's attention to the billboard. After reading the inscription, he became momentarily silent then said, 'do you know who I'm thinking about now?'

'It's got to be me of course,' replied Emily jocularly.

'Those words make me think of Bruce and Natasha.'

'Good heavens! I haven't thought of them in ages. Natasha stopped phoning me a long time ago and I haven't seen her since that first night in your house. She never answers whenever I've tried phoning her. So tell me more about them. Did they get on well afterwards?'

'After that night in my house, they started going out together. Bruce moved to Austria and Natasha joined him there, but they only stayed for three months before coming back to the UK. Then Bruce travelled to Rotterdam and Natasha stayed in the UK. They were talking about getting married in the future . . .'

'This is very interesting. I'm all ears,' said Emily.

'After Bruce left for the Netherlands, Natasha began to work for a charity organization in London. She was sent on an assignment to Bangkok in Thailand, where she met a Thai university professor and they fell in love. She converted to Buddhism and married the man, then sent an email to Bruce telling him what she'd done.'

'So she's in Thailand now?'

'I suppose so. Her email so devastated Bruce that he had a nervous breakdown. He had to return to the UK and since then he's been in and out of psychiatric hospitals.'

'What a tragic end to a love affair that had all the potential to bring joy to both of them,' said Emily. They had been queuing at the garage all this time, but now Richard fuelled up the car and they drove off again.

'So much for that innocent-looking billboard. It triggered off a story you hadn't known about,' said Richard.

'Could this be the reason why Natasha has been avoiding me? I never knew all this before. I wish her and her husband good luck.'

'Anyway, let's change the subject. When would you like to go out for dinner at Griffiths Restaurant?'

'We could go tomorrow evening. I love the ambience there.'

'When we get home, can you check your diary to make sure that you won't be on-call in two weeks' time?'

'Why, what's going to happen then?'

'I'll tell you when we get home. I know that you like romantic surprises.'

As Richard continued driving, Emily thought about how happy and relieved she had been not to have to carry on working at Royal Infirmary when she broke up with Burnty. She felt that it was a blessed coincidence and imagined how she would have coped with hospital gossip and how delighted the nurse who used to torment her would have been. She bore Burnty no ill-will

whatsoever and still considered him to be a friend, though probably not one that she would be seeing for a long time. As she
contemplated all this, Richard negotiated the bend that finally
led to their house.

18

October 2004

Burnty was on a train on his way to Swansea. It had been almost a year since he broke up with Emily. He had followed the advice that Dominic had given him in the immediate aftermath of the break up. He had travelled to the USA to visit Robert and from there he went to Nigeria to see his parents, his other siblings and their respective families. His family had all been very supportive when they learnt about his break up with Emily. They had prayed for him and reassured him that he would eventually find his life partner and that whatever belonged to him would eventually come to him.

Burnty's trips had succeeded in calming his frayed nerves and he felt much better when he left Nigeria for the UK. It was almost like a miracle to him when he met Anonsa at Heathrow Airport, he had never imagined that he would set his eyes on her again. Not only did he now have a new girlfriend, he had just taken up his appointment as a specialist registrar at the Whittington Hospital in London. The house he had shared with Emily had been sold, which made their break-up seem much more final. This greatly helped Burnty to put the affair behind him. He did not hold a grudge against Emily, knowing full well that love can never be forced; it has to be freely given. Every human being has the right to go wherever his or her heart takes them. He would have been happy to continue his relationship with Emily but things hadn't worked out that way, and he was moving on with his life. He realized that the hand of fate has a big role to play in all our lives. Change might seem very difficult to bear initially, but sometimes it is the harbinger of good things to come.

As Burnty thought philosophically about what was happening in his life, an announcement told him that the train was only thirty minutes away from Swansea. He phoned Anonsa to tell her that he'd be there soon, then began to think about his younger brother, Robert. He had been very supportive when Burnty visited him and told him that Emily had left him. Robert was in a stable relationship with an African-American woman from Atlanta. Burnty also found himself thinking about his new place of work. Soon afterwards, the train came to a final stop at Swansea station and all the passengers disembarked.

As Burnty made his way onto the platform he spotted Anonsa from afar. As he walked towards her, she spotted him too and rushed towards him and embraced him. They hugged and kissed then walked together to Anonsa's car.

'I hope you haven't been waiting for too long?' said Burnty.

'No. I've only been waiting for about ten minutes. How was the journey?'

'It was very interesting, this being my first time in Wales.'

'I rarely get the time to travel around locally except when I go on courses away from the hospital.'

'Swansea seems to be a lovely city,' said Burnty, as they drove through the city centre on their way to Anonsa's house.

'It is; and the train station is nice and easy to get to.'

When they arrived at Anonsa's house, she parked the car and helped Burnty to carry his bags in from the car. When they were inside the house and had shut the door behind them, they kissed each other warmly. Tears began to roll down Anonsa's cheeks as she was overcome by emotion and Burnty had to try harder to hold back his own tears.

'The Lord is wonderful. I never imagined that we could be together again,' said Anonsa, as she wiped her tears.

Burnty held her hand. 'This is God's choice, how else can it be explained? So let's work at it and enjoy it,' he said.

As Burnty made himself comfortable on the sofa in the sitting room, Anonsa went into the kitchen to collect the food she had already prepared and carried it into the dining room. When she had finished setting the table she invited Burnty to join her and they ate together in the dining room.

'You are such a fantastic cook. What a delicious meal!' said Burnty genuinely.

'Thank you.'

As they ate they reminisced over the past and what had happened to them. They both steered clear of the topic of their most recent relationships like the plague. When they finished eating they sat together in the lounge and watched TV. After a while Anonsa excused herself and went for a shower. She came back to join Burnty wearing a silk negligee which revealed her stunning figure.

'Would you like a shower?' asked Anonsa, smiling as she rubbed Burnty's back.

Burnty smiled back and then went to have a shower. He came back wearing a velvety dressing gown. It was very late in the evening. Being the weekend they didn't have to worry about work the following day, so they continued to watch the TV and chat.

As midnight approached they began to kiss and fondle each other. Soon they were hurrying upstairs to bed feeling heated up with passion. On reaching the bedroom, they undressed and began to make love as if they had been doing this together every day of their lives. Yet, this was their first time making love together. They both cried out in delight as their lovemaking became more energetic and impassioned.

Burnty and Anonsa woke up the following morning feeling very happy.

'Only God could have made this happen. We were expelled for something which we never did, but God has ordained that it is our destiny to come together and we've done that now,' said Anonsa, sounding very emotional.

'It's quite clear now that God has always wanted us to be together and it is true that two people God has put together no man shall put asunder,' said Burnty.

Before Anonsa could respond, Burnty took a ring from the pocket of his dressing gown and bent down on one knee to propose to her. Anonsa was completely stupefied by the gesture. She accepted readily and hugged him and they kissed each other and collapsed in bed together. Anonsa then began to sing one of her favourite love songs and Burnty joined in intermittently whenever she sang a part with which he was familiar.

'That is one of my favourite songs,' said Anonsa.

'I never knew that you could sing so well,' said Burnty. 'I think you should be in a choir.'

'I'm already a member of my church choir and I performed at the last Christmas festival. I'll want you to come and watch me at this year's Christmas celebration.'

'I can't wait to see my darling thrill the world with her mellifluous voice.' Burnty looked besotted. When they went down to the sitting room, Anonsa continued singing until she was interrupted by her cell phone ringing. 'Hello, this is Anonsa.'

'Hi Anonsa, I know its been ages but I just wanted to return your phone call. I'm sorry it's taken me so long.' It was Anonsa's friend Theresa.

'Hi Theresa. How nice to hear your voice again. Never mind, I knew that you must be busy with work and family commitments. It's always lovely to talk to you. How's work and your family?'

'My work is going well, and my family are doing fine thank you.'

'That's great. How about your parents?'

'They're alright. My dad has recently returned from Lagos where he was representing Oxfam at the Annual Youth Event of The Homij And Tanassah Foundation for World Peace. He said that he met the patroness of that foundation who was a pleasant lady, who told him that her daughter was a doctor in the UK.'

'That was my mum, Mrs Susan Omiyale.'

'Gosh! What an amazing coincidence. He didn't know that she was your mum. I can't wait to tell him that he's met your mum without knowing it. He'll be delighted.'

'This shows that we truly live in a global village.'

'I think it is good for the world. The more people from different parts of the world who meet, the more tolerant and less xenophobic they'll become.'

'I agree with you. I always enjoy our conversations so much. I must say that I've missed talking to you recently.'

'Do you have guests in your house? I can hear voices in the background.'

'The sound is actually coming from the TV but you're right,

I do have a guest. My new fiancé is here. I don't think that you've met each other yet, but I'll let you speak to him,' said Anonsa. She handed the handset to Burnty and told him that it was her friend, Theresa.

'Hello, my name is Burnty. Anonsa has spoken about you. She told me that you were close friends and that you worked together in Dundee.'

'That's true. How are you, and what do you do?'

'I'm doing fine. I work in Whittington Hospital in London as a specialist registrar in oral and maxillofacial surgery.'

'That's nice. I hope you are enjoying it there.'

'Well, I try to.'

'We all do. It's nice speaking to you. I wish you success in your work.'

'Thank you. Best wishes to you too. Let me hand you back to Anonsa,' said Burnty.

'Anonsa, I mustn't keep you on the phone for too long. I'm pleased to know that you are doing well. I'll continue to keep in touch.'

'Thank you so much, Theresa. You're such a wonderful friend. Please send my regards to your husband, kids and parents,' said Anonsa. They said goodbye and hung up.

'It's always good to be in touch with friends. We all need other human beings; no man is an island, as the saying goes,' said Burnty.

'That's very true.'

Anonsa later went into the kitchen to prepare a meal for them. When it was ready they ate and chatted together. Afterwards they jumped into Anonsa's car and went for a drive round the city. By the time they came back home it was time for Burnty to leave for London.

19

December 2004

It had been almost two months since Burnty proposed to Anonsa. They were both very happy about their relationship and their respective families were now aware of it and they were very pleased too. Burnty and Anonsa did not want to waste too much time before getting married. They had already fixed a date and had been negotiating with a printer for the printing of the invitations. The wording on the cards had initially caused a few problems, but this had been resolved, and the invitations now read:

You are cordially invited to the wedding ceremony between,
our son,
BURNTY AKPAN CHRISTOPHER
and our daughter,
ANONSA PELU OMIYALE

The Islington Registry Office in London had been chosen as the venue for the civil ceremony, while the reception was to follow at St Mary's Church Hall in West London. Susan was very happy about her daughter's impending wedding ceremony. She had been particularly worried about Anonsa's break-up with her former boyfriend, but she had never allowed the depth of her anxiety to show because she thought it might exacerbate Anonsa's feelings of gloom. Especially since Anonsa's twin younger brothers in America were both happily married with children of their own. Susan had always prayed for Anonsa and firmly believed that her time would come. She was very supportive when she found out that Burnty was the person with whom her daughter had been expelled from High School. This knowledge only served to strengthen her belief in fate and destiny. Burnty's parents were also very supportive and both families had since met one another.

The preparations for the wedding were at an advanced stage. The invitations had been sent out, and the bookings for the venues had been confirmed. Burnty's and Anonsa's families in Nigeria had been informed and many of them had already made their travel arrangements.

It was drizzling outside as the cars made their way to the Islington Registry Office. It was Burnty's and Anonsa's wedding day. Many of the guests had already arrived. When Anonsa and Burnty arrived, the marriage ceremony began. Everyone present watched them in admiration as the ceremony progressed. For those who were already married, the occasion reminded them of their own wedding day while, those who were yet to tie the nuptial knot looked forward to doing so in the future. The brief ceremony was soon over. After the photographs Anonsa and Burnty, now a married couple, were whisked off to St Mary's Church Hall in West London in a white limousine for their wedding reception.

The venue had been amply decorated with flowers. Burnty's

cousin, Dominic, had been his best man while Anonsa's matron of honour had been her close friend Theresa. As the bride and groom entered the church hall they were surrounded by an ambience of calm, as the beautiful background music pierced everyone's heart. They looked like a match made in heaven, with smiles of hope and optimism flashing on their faces. After the reception was over there was plenty of food and drink. Anonsa and Burnty were then driven off in the white limousine as husband and wife stepping into the uncertain waters of married life.

Passengers were boarding the British Airways Boeing 747 bound for Faro in the Algarve as it sat on the tarmac at Heathrow Airport. As the passengers climbed onto the aircraft their faces radiated happiness and excitement. Two of the passengers were Anonsa and Burnty, who were going to Portugal for their honeymoon.

As the aircraft took off Burnty heaved a sigh and said, 'Here we go, what God has joined together . . .'

'Let no man put asunder,' cut in Anonsa.

They then held each other's hand and kissed as the aircraft rose into the air.